Jones watched her move with assurance to the donkey to unload a small cooler.

That didn't seem very Wild West, as he'd imagined it as a boy. But they weren't in the Wild West. They had cell phones and sunscreen.

He turned back to the wall. His archaeologist's interest was piqued. He heard Lavonda talking to their donkey, but he didn't catch what she said because he'd noticed something else. Accessing his flashlight app, he shone it into the cave's dark corners.

"What did you find?" Lavonda's hushed voice whispered over his skin.

"Probably nothing, but I saw... Ahh, just there." He pointed.

Lavonda moved closer, and a shiver of awareness skittered through him. Distracted, he let the flashlight beam swing wildly.

"Did you see something?" She touched his forearm briefly, her small fingers leaving a heated impression.

"Not yet," he said calmly, as though he was in a lecture hall and not standing next to an enchanted pixie, a *leannán sí* out of a Scottish fairy tale. He concentrated on the beam of light and what had caught his eye.

"There it is."

Dear Reader,

Welcome to Angel Crossing, Arizona—my new series set in a fictional town filled with heart and humor. It's fitting that the first book in this series is about two people finding their way home. Lavonda Leigh (who showed up in both *The Surgeon and the Cowgirl* and *The Convenient Cowboy*) is back to being a cowgirl after years in the corporate world, and Scottish archaeologist Jones Kincaid is combing the desert for ancient treasure to save his career. These two never planned to stick around Angel Crossing, but they soon discover what home is in Arizona's wide-open spaces and their own warm embraces.

Despite a very German name, I have quite a bit of Scots in my background and have traveled to the country of haggis and kilts a number of times. Something in the Scottish take on life reminds me of the cowboy attitude. Arizona is even home to an annual Highland games, which I've included in this book.

As my new series gets started off with a bagpipe and a yee-haw, I am already working on other stories of the men and women in Angel Crossing. No matter their backgrounds, they each find their place in this town that embraces change while staying true to its heart. Quite a feat.

If you want to know more about my inspirations and musings or want to drop me a note, check out my website and blog at heidihormel.net, where you also can sign up for my newsletter. Or connect with me at Facebook.com/authorheidihormel; Twitter.com/heidihormel; or Pinterest.com/hhormel.

Yee-haw,

Heidi Hormel

THE ACCIDENTAL COWBOY

Heidi Hormel

HARLEQUIN® AMERICAN ROMANCE®

Recycling programs
for this product may
not exist in your area.

ISBN-13: 978-0-373-75616-2

The Accidental Cowboy

Copyright © 2016 by Heidi Hormel

Printed in U.S.A.

With stints as an innkeeper, radio talk show host and craft store manager, **Heidi Hormel** settled into her true calling as a writer by spending years as a reporter (covering the story of the rampaging elephants Debbie and Tina) and as a PR flunky (staying calm in the face of Cookiegate). Now she is happiest penning romances with a wink and a wiggle.

A small-town girl from the Snack Food Capital of the World, Heidi has trotted over a good portion of the globe, from Tombstone in Arizona to Loch Ness in Scotland to the depths of Death Valley. She draws on all of these experiences for her books, especially for her Angel Crossing, Arizona series.

Heidi is on the web at heidihormel.net, as well as socially out there at Facebook.com/authorheidihormel; Twitter.com/heidihormel; and Pinterest.com/hhormel.

Books by Heidi Hormel

Harlequin American Romance

The Surgeon and the Cowgirl
The Convenient Cowboy

For the wonderfully amazing young men
who allowed me to borrow their names
and never complained.

Chapter One

"Yep. He's got the arms for it," remarked the old woman, munching a churro and nodding down at the arena filled with kilts, kneesocks and T-shirts. Last week it had been bulls, broncs and cowboys.

The flash of a hairy leg and a swirling kilt didn't excite Lavonda Leigh any more than the rest of her life did right now. She checked her phone for messages, a habit from working in corporate communications, where she'd been expected to be available 24-7. She glanced back at the ring, trying to decide which one of the men was the egghead she'd have to babysit for the community college that owned the ranch she'd been calling home. Even though Professor McNerdy would be staying at the ranch, too, they'd barely see each other because she lived in the cozy and private in-law quarters added in the 1970s to the rear of the hacienda-style house. Plus, he'd be out poking around the desert looking for ancient beans—that had to be the most boring research topic. A topic she was glad she didn't have to spin into PR gold.

"That's it. Next time you should watch and not text," the other woman said with disapproval.

Lavonda ignored her and started down the metal

bleachers to find the Scottish professor, who had insisted that he compete in the local Highland games with the college's team. The group should've been easy to find in the sea of plaid. They'd be the ones in glasses with sunken chests and spindly arms. Judgmental? Yep. But she'd grown up with cowboys, and a bunch of academics just didn't cut it in the he-man department.

Lavonda moved along with the small crowd. Were there Highland-game groupies, like rodeo-buckle bunnies? She finally saw the college's distinctive lime-green canopy, shading a group of kilted men. No spindly arms, though. Maybe they were ringers. Did Highland games have ringers?

"Excuse me," she said, raising her voice to be heard over the manly rounds of congratulations. "I'm here to pick up Professor Kincaid."

A juvenile *ooh* went through the assembled men. She shook her head. They sounded just like her brother and his friends, somewhere around junior high in emotional and social maturity.

"Hey, Jones," a bearded behemoth shouted over his shoulder, "you've got a groupie."

The others laughed and lifted their bottles of beer. Right. This was why cowboys had stopped appealing to her, despite their tight jeans, tilted hats and dusty shirts. Men plus beer equaled jerks.

"Just a moment," a voice said from the other side of the shelter. "Must get my bag."

She peered through the throng. Being short made that a little difficult since each man appeared to be the height of one of the logs they'd tossed. Really, what was the point of throwing a tree?

"Good afternoon, Ms. Leigh." The voice was deep, with a Ewan McGregor accent.

A man nearly a foot taller than her, with arms and chest appropriately large enough to toss all the things that had just been tossed, strode over. He looked at her with eyes the deep, dark green of a ponderosa pine. "Lavonda," she said automatically, holding out a hand and smiling. *They must grow them big in Scotland.* "It's a pleasure to meet you."

Another chorus of masculine comments, including "That's what she said," which didn't make any sense. This group might be more elementary school than junior high.

"I'm ready," he said, trying to rearrange his longer-than-it-should-be auburn hair, a color just like a bay horse her dad had owned.

"I'll say it so you guys don't have to," Lavonda said to the crowd of academics. "'That's what she said.'"

The professor looked down at her and squinted a little before leaning forward and whispering, "What does that mean? They've been saying that and I can't quite—"

"I'll explain in the car. You only have the one bag?"

"The others are being delivered." He easily lifted the large duffel at his feet. His arm bulged nicely. No. Not nicely, Lavonda told herself. This was the man she was babysitting, nothing more.

LAVONDA HAD NEVER felt her Mini Cooper was small until Professor Kincaid—no, she was supposed to call him Jones—had wedged himself inside. Why hadn't she brought the ranch pickup? They still had another thirty minutes or more stuck in her vehicle.

"You study beans, right?" she asked, hoping this conversation would go better than her attempts to explain "that's what she said."

"Yes. By examining the usage of foodstuffs, we can discern…"

He went on, but her brain had hit the pleasant autopilot where she could nod as needed without actually listening. "I'm sorry. What did you say?" From the silence, she knew she'd missed something.

"I asked about the other transportation at the ranch."

"An old pickup, three horses and a donkey," she said, glancing over at him and catching a look of annoyance.

"I need to make a call," he said, and pulled a cell phone from the furry sporran, aka Scottish man-purse, which previously she'd only ever seen on someone dressed up at Halloween.

She'd been dismissed. She'd gotten used to it working with the movers and shakers in her corporate jobs, but that didn't stop her from being miffed. She watched the road, ignoring the nearness of her passenger, the familiar odor of sweaty male combined with Jones's own scent of dusty wool and cool, dark earth. She did not, however, find it sexy. Sexy to her nearly thirty-year-old self included a tailored jacket, starched shirt and silk tie, like Harvey Specter from *Suits*.

She glanced over, thinking his hair was too long and his prickly jaw too sharp. He was also too tall, probably even taller than her brother, Danny. Why had she gotten the short genes?

"I understand that you will be providing meals?"

That was news to her, but she'd promised her friend Gwen, the president of the college, she'd keep this man happy—within reason. "I can certainly do that," she said calmly, while she scrambled to remember what food she had at the house.

"Then we will not need to stop for supplies."

"Not unless there's something specific that you like or need. The ranch isn't close to any stores."

"I am certain what you have will be fine until I get settled. I flew in this morning, and jet lag is catching up with me."

"What? You went right from the airport to the stadium?"

"The team would have had to forfeit. If I hadn't been here, then they would have been out of the running for the regional competition."

She looked at him more closely. He did look a little droopy around the eyes. "I'll make something quick for dinner."

"Wonderful."

She nodded and added, "I've moved into the in-law quarters. You'll have the house to yourself."

"That will work fine, although I plan to be in the field the majority of the time."

"You do have a hat and sunscreen, right?"

"I'm not a tenderfoot." He reached easily into the backseat and dug in his bag, pulling out a battered straw cowboy hat.

She hadn't expected that.

"What?" Jones asked. "We've heard of cowboys in Scotland. This hat has been on every dig with me."

"Surprised it's made it this far. Jammed into your bag. Is that any way to treat it?"

He tilted the hat. "I didn't want to forget it. It's my lucky hat."

She grinned, thinking, *That's what she said.* Professional, she reminded herself. Make small talk. "Did you find that in London or have you been west before?"

"Edinburgh has its own Wild West street in Morningside."

"I'd never have imagined. Is that where you became interested in Arizona and beans?"

His expression froze. "Something like that."

He was lying. Why would he lie about that? Crap. She'd nearly missed the turnoff for the ranch. "Not long now," she said, glancing over at the kilted giant in his cowboy hat. "Well, if you want to go to a rodeo or ride the range, let me know. I've got connections." Connections that she'd mostly severed long ago, right after winning the teen bronc riding championship, but her brother or dad would show him around if she asked…nicely. Of course, then she'd be grilled about what she planned to do with her life. Right now, get this man home and into bed—that's what she said.

LAVONDA LED HIM into the long, low, mud-colored ranch house, explaining that it had been on the property for nearly one hundred years. She acted as if that were a great deal of time. He didn't point out the "new" part of his family home had been built before Arizona was even a territory.

"It doesn't look like they've dropped off your other stuff," she said as she opened the front door. "The delivery guys just leave whatever here on the front porch. The woman who built the house was originally from Georgia and insisted a house wasn't a home without a porch, although she probably called it a 'veranda.'"

He stepped into the dim house, feeling taller than usual. The ceilings didn't soar and the pixie of a woman who, he'd been told, cared for the property barely reached his shoulder. His nose twitched. "Is that a cat?" he accused, pointing at a feline that was wider than it was tall.

"Um…yeah?" Lavonda said as she kept moving despite the cat's yowl.

"Get it out."

"Excuse me? That's Cat."

"I bloody well know it's a cat." He sneezed. "No one told me you had a bloody cat."

"The cat's name is Cat. Why would anyone tell you about her?"

"Because I'm allergic." Usually cats just made him sneeze. He hadn't had a full-blown asthma attack since he was a child. He stumbled outside where the desert heat hit him like an anvil in one of those American coyote cartoons. He leaned over and made himself breathe slowly out and in. The stress and jet lag had laid him low, obviously.

"Should I call nine-one-one?" Lavonda asked, her dark eyes even wider than usual.

He shook his head. "I'll be fine in a moment, but you need to remove that animal." The damned thing had followed them outside. He stepped away. It followed him, trying to rub against his stockinged leg. Dignity be damned, he danced away and batted at the feline.

"Cat," Lavonda said, reaching forward, snatching up her pet and dumping it in the yard.

"Has that animal been living in the house?" He'd have to dose himself with antihistamines. Good thing he'd be out in the field soon.

"She usually hangs out in the barn with Reese. They are in one of those weird different-species friendships."

Damn it. Why couldn't one thing go smoothly today? Just one bleedin' thing? "My allergy medication is in the cases that have not been delivered. We'll need to take a trip to the shops after all." His eyes itched, but he refused to give in and rub them. He should be right as rain with over-the-counter tablets.

Her frown quickly turned it into a smile. "Sure. Anything else? Maybe you should check the fridge to see what we're missing."

His stash of Hobnob biscuits was in the other luggage, too. This sort of day called for a pint and his favorite oat biscuits—or should he say cookies now that he was in the US? Why had he thought flying all night followed by an afternoon at the games would be a good idea? Because he was an ass, his brother would say. Actually, it was even worse. He'd mixed up the dates and thought the games were next week. When he'd figured out the mistake, it'd been too late to back out.

"Check the fridge, then we'll run to the store," Lavonda said with a patient smile.

He sneezed. Damned cat.

BY THE TIME they got back to the ranch, he was so tired that even the dusty ground in front of the house looked comfortable. On top of the jet lag, the medicine had made him drowsy and a little dizzy. Though that may have been from lack of food. He should have let her talk him into stopping at the caravan parked beside the road in town. She'd said it had the best tamales and fry bread. He'd just been too tired. He wanted a bed now. "Which is my room?"

"Any, really. They all have linens—"

He didn't wait for her to finish, going to the nearest room and dropping his duffel on the floor, followed by his shirt, shoes, stockings and kilt. He should take a shower. He had a rank odor of travel and competition about him. Tomorrow. He'd do that tomorrow. He stepped forward, looked down and stopped.

"Lavonda." He choked out the name, totally awake now. "Ms. Leigh." His voice finally reached an adequate volume.

"Yes," she said tentatively as she knocked on the door. "What did you need?"

"Come in, please." He didn't take his eyes from the creature on his foot.

"Did you forget to get something at the store? It'll have to wait until tomorrow. Damn," she said suddenly with feeling. "It didn't get you, did it?"

"No."

"Good. The sting won't kill you, but it hurts like

heck. Let me think a second." She stepped completely into the bedroom.

His foot twitched all on its own, and the mammoth insect moved. "It would seem logical that the job of caretaker include ensuring all vermin have been eliminated?" *Good, Jones, upset the one person who can help you.* Maybe he could just kick out his foot, except now the beast had scrambled onto his ankle.

LAVONDA STARED AT the nasty, pissed-off bug as the TV news crawl flashed through her mind: Scottish professor killed by rogue scorpion as caretaker does nothing. She could stamp on it. No. It had moved up his leg toward—she'd keep her gaze from moving farther up his almost naked body. "Don't move."

"I had not planned to. Maybe you could swat it away with a stick?"

That was a good suggestion. She looked around the room. Nothing here. "I'll be right back."

"Certainly."

He was pale, though she wasn't sure if that was a usual lack-of-sun complexion or the bug on his foot. She had to admit it took balls—no, that was wrong. It took courage to stand still like that. She looked at the courage in question… What was her problem? The man could die… Okay, probably not from a scorpion, but still. She had started out of the room, when Cat came streaking in, howling like an animal possessed.

"What the bloody—"

"Cat," she yelled as the animal landed on his foot, batting the bug away and then pouncing on it like the puma she apparently thought she was. With a triumphant meow, she squashed the scorpion. The professor sneezed. Cat sat, looking regal and pleased above the mess of bug innards.

"I guess I don't need that stick," Lavonda said lamely. "Cat saved you."

She looked up from Cat and her prey. Jones stood in just his underwear, limned in gold from the last rays of the setting sun as it sparked off the hairs on his arms and legs, all of him very fit and substantial.

"Perhaps…" He sniffed loudly, then sneezed.

"Of course," she said, and as she lunged forward to get Cat, she brushed against—oh my, that wasn't his thigh. That was his courage. She looked up into his watering and surprised eyes. "Sorry?" Only she wasn't. Crap. The body part in question seemed to be ignoring the fact that he had just narrowly avoided death. She scurried back. He turned and groped on the floor for his kilt. He wrapped it around his waist and buckled it on. He didn't have anything to be embarrassed about…

She snatched up Cat. "I'll be back to clean up the mess," she mumbled as she hurried from the room. She wasn't a blusher, but she knew her face was flaming.

Cat yowled and Lavonda loosened her death grip on the animal as she entered the dimness of the barn. It's where Cat usually hung out with Reese, the miniature donkey. And now that Cat had found her inner killing machine, she could take care of the mice that were eating their weight in grain.

"Cat, stay here," she told the soccer ball–shaped feline. "Professor McNerdy can't take you, so you need to hang here, which you like better anyway." Cat walked away, her tail straight up in the air and swaying slowly in contempt.

The three horses popped their heads over the stalls, hopeful for a treat, and Reese brayed loudly, smacking his stall with a tiny hoof to get some feline love. Cat ignored him and sat licking her paws. The poor miniature donkey didn't understand that cats did what they wanted, when they wanted, and the more you wanted them to do something the less likely they were to do it.

How long did she need to wait out here until she and the professor could both pretend that she hadn't felt up his bucking bronc, accidental or not. Awkward with a capital *A*. She should think about how to make him feel welcome after this disaster. She cared for the property and the animals in exchange for staying rent free at the ranch. Humans were animals, after all, so it was her job to take care of him. She'd get back to writing press releases and taking calls from MSNBC soon enough. She might even be missing the pressure cooker of corporate work.

"Yowl," Cat said, looking at her accusingly with her slightly crossed Siamese-blue eyes. She nosed an empty food bowl into Lavonda's foot. Good distraction. She focused on Cat. "If I feed you this time, you promise to take care of the mice and stay away from the professor, right?"

Cat meowed again and batted the food bowl. Lavonda should've been the one promising to leave the professor alone. She dug out the plastic container where she kept the cat's kibble. A big hole had been chewed in it and a mouse looked up from the bottom, holding a piece of food with a mousy laugh.

Chapter Two

"Damn it," Jones said into his mobile two days after landing at the ranch from hell. "What do you mean you can't make it for another month?"

"Just what I said," replied the experienced guide, the one who had his payment in full.

"What about the money?"

"I'll return it."

"I had bloody well better see that money back in my account within the week."

"Seeing as how that account is in England—"

"Scotland."

"Whatever. It may just take extra time. No reason to blow a gasket."

"I will expect the funds in the account within the week. I know you know how because you asked for me to electronically transfer the cash in the first place."

"You see—"

"I don't want excuses. I expect the money returned. If I must get a solicitor involved—"

"This ain't Nevada, and I never had to pay for *that*."

What was the man babbling about? Then his brain

made the connection. "A solicitor is an attorney. I did not mean paying for sex." Maybe he was fortunate this man could not guide him after all. "What?"

"I said now that I think on it, I'm pretty certain the contract said no refunds."

"I can't imagine that would hold up in court, since you are in breach of the contract."

"Whatever. I can't take ya." The line went dead.

What the hell could he do now? He'd suspected there was a problem when he had been unable to reach his allegedly professional guide. He'd made assumptions about the man's abilities and reliability. He should have done more research, and he would have if this had been one of his usual research trips. So much more than the discovery of a little piece of an academic puzzle was riding on it.

He squinted against the sun and put the mobile back in his pocket. He'd come outside to get a better signal and to ensure there was absolutely no chance Lavonda could overhear him, no matter if she was in her own rooms. He had to be discreet about exactly where he was going and what he was doing. As far as both universities understood, the bulk of his research would investigate the Hohokam and their use of beans as an alternate source of protein, and would not involve looking for a long-lost treasure. Jones could, using a local satnav system, probably go forward with his work. He'd wanted a local guide so he didn't run afoul of either the US government or the local Native American tribes. His recent string of bad luck had him on edge.

This secret expedition had to end well. In the course of his usual life, Jones would have dismissed the journals he'd found, purportedly from an early-twentieth-century Kincaid home here in Arizona. He wasn't living his usual life, though. Everything had unraveled when his big find, the one that should have gotten him full status at the university, as well as a chairmanship, had led to a cairn filled with discarded, valueless children's toys. Unearthing the fabled Kincaid's Cache with its statuary and gold would redeem him in more ways than one.

If looking for agricultural evidence was the only thing on his agenda, he'd have just called the university for a new guide. He couldn't afford any extra scrutiny of his expedition, especially from his brother.

"Something wrong?" Lavonda asked, strolling from the back of the house, her head tilted to the side and the bright sun sparking off her sleek fall of hair.

"No," he said, drawing out the word as his mind turned over potential solutions.

"Hmm...well, you might not want to stand in the sun without a hat. Do you have on sunscreen?" Her wide-eyed gaze scanned him up and down with clinical interest.

"I'm fine." Not only would he have to rely on his own satnav system if hared off on his own, the guide had promised to bring the transport.

"You leave tomorrow, right? For how long?"

"A change of plans. I won't be leaving tomorrow."

"So when will you be going?"

"That is yet to be determined."

She frowned. "Humph." It was a little pixie snort. How could he think that was cute, even endearing? Maybe he did need a hat.

"There's a colleague I must ring," he lied, to move her along.

"I'm going out to check one of the Hohokam sites. You'll be okay here on your own?"

He couldn't decide what she was trying to imply. "Absolutely. What site?"

"One with petroglyphs and a couple of metate corn grinders. Part of my duties as caretaker. I go out and make sure nothing has been damaged or needs stabilization. It's a restricted area, but there have been problems in the past. I also keep my eyes on the saguaros. The big ones get rustled."

Did she want him to come with her? Did he want to go? Yes, he decided. It would be better than second-guessing his just-this-minute decision to explore on his own. In fact, going out with her would be a good way to get the lay of the land. "Why don't I come with you? The metates could be associated with the bean culture." The more he thought about it, the better this decision became. He could use his own satnav for coordinates if he saw any of the landmarks noted in the journal.

"It'll be pretty boring, and I'm walking."

"I'm used to physical activity."

"Walking in the desert is not tossing trees."

He ignored her comment. "I'll need to change footwear and get my lucky hat."

She sighed heavily. "Don't forget the sunscreen."

Maybe the guide canceling wasn't part of his curse. Could his luck be changing?

"WHAT IS THAT?" Jones asked Lavonda, pointing at Reese. The tiny donkey's long ears drooped and his stubby brush tail flicked at an imaginary fly.

"This is our pack mule…well, burro." Lavonda patted the animal. She didn't want his feelings hurt. He might only be as tall as a good-sized Great Dane, but he had the ego of a Clydesdale.

Jones's face went from annoyed to amused and back to annoyed, but he said nothing. She'd already noticed that he was standoffish, not unlike the executives she'd worked with as a highly paid corporate communications specialist. She could suck it up and be nice. She'd definitely learned to do it before.

"You'll thank Reese when we unpack the water and snacks. Plus, this little guy needs the exercise and experience." She clucked to get the burro moving. She heard the scuff of Jones's boots following them. "Did you know that saguaro cacti only grow in the Sonoran Desert and the arms don't appear until the plant is about seventy years old?"

"Yes. As part of my preparations for this trip, I did internet research on the region."

Not friendly but factual. She could live with that.

"Your…what did you call it?" He gestured at her pack animal.

"Reese. And he's a he…or was a he."

"Is he a native of the region?"

She went on to explain how burros, aka donkeys, were used by miners and then turned loose to become feral. Reese had descended from those intrepid little animals. "My sister, Jessie, has a therapeutic riding program for children with medical challenges. She's considering burros for cart work."

"Cart work?"

"Pulling children in carts or buggies. Especially the younger kids who may be too small to ride a pony.

The burros' size also makes them less intimidating. They're very, very smart and affectionate."

"He doesn't seem like the type of beast a cowgirl like you would defend."

"I'm not a *real* cowgirl. Not anymore." She closed her mouth fast. She didn't want to talk about this with a stranger.

"You live in Arizona on a ranch, and—"

"That doesn't make you a cowgirl," she shot back. What the hell? She knew how to keep quiet even when provoked. She'd been the spokeswoman when her company had been at the center of a media crap storm, and she hadn't let the press rattle her. Here she was ready to lose her cool with a professor studying beans. She turned to Reese and gave herself a moment to relax. This man was from Scotland. Of course he didn't understand that being a cowgirl was more than a hat and boots.

"Are you sure your burro is up to this outing?"

She refocused on small talk. "Reese learned that looking pathetic would get him out of work with his last owner. The college just recently received the property as a bequest. He and Cat came with it. There's a goat, too, but she's out eating her weight in tumbleweeds."

"Quite a menagerie."

"At least we don't have a javelina."

"Are they related to scorpions?" he asked straight-faced, though she could see that he was trying to… flirt? No way.

"My friend Olympia's stepson rescued one and called it Petunia. You know, like the pig in the cartoon? Except they're not pigs, even though people

call them wild pigs. They're peccaries, a big rodent…
sort of."

"Your friend allowed her stepson to adopt a rat?"

She had to smile at that. Petunia and all javelinas
looked like hairy, long-nosed pigs. "Much cuter than
any rat I've ever seen, especially Petunia. I'm sure
she's back in the wild by now. That was their agreement. Actually, in the wild, they can be a problem,
especially the boars that get very aggressive."

"Any other deadly creatures? Or ones that are
called one thing but are really another?"

"Most wild things run when they see or smell a
human." She looked at the familiar pile of boulders.
"We'll need to go up there. That's where the rock
drawings I need to check are."

"The petroglyphs," he corrected.

"The *petroglyphs* are scattered throughout the
area, along with metates." Did he think she was stupid because she had breasts?

He hummed an answer, squinting up at the outcropping. "This region has been inhabited for more
than two thousand years. The people created the necessary irrigation techniques. There are indications
of widespread agriculture." He sounded so stilted.
"Perhaps I'll see evidence of bean production in the
drawings."

Really, who studied beans? Men like Jones did,
along with a number of the faculty her friend and
president of the college Gwen had introduced her to.
That's when Gwen had asked Lavonda to work her
PR magic in addition to her caretaking duties. Gwen
hoped a little notice by the press of the Angel Crossing campus would lead to better funding. The profes-

sors and researchers had tunnel vision when it came to their fields of study. She was glad she didn't have to try to make his bean research interesting to the general public.

"Perhaps," she finally said.

"You said this area is protected? By the college?"

They continued their way up the slope on the barely discernable path. "The ranch house has national historic landmark status. The college had been approached about protecting the acreage with a federal designation."

"Why would the ranch be considered 'historic'?"

Could the man get more annoying? Or maybe he was really interested in the answer. She looked at him closely. His head was cocked a little to the side and softness curved his lips. Not that she was looking all that closely. "After the woman from Georgia, it was owned by Arizona's first 'official' cowgirl. She might have beat out Annie Oakley if they'd ever met."

"That's quite a claim, from what I understand."

"I've seen the stats and the pictures. She was good. She had a way with horses, too. She could ride anything, even competed as a bareback bronc rider... when the cowboys would let her." Lavonda said. "When I was competing, she was the kind of cowgirl I was trying to live up to, not afraid to go up against the boys." She shut up, not sure why all of that had come spilling out. No one wanted to hear her own ancient history.

"You rode broncs?" He looked more than a little surprised.

"You only have to hold on."

"I believe there's more to it than that."

"Not much, and being short was an advantage. Low center of gravity."

"Interesting," he said with a crooked smiled, then asked with an eye on the donkey, "Is there a problem with the burro?"

She pulled on Reese's rope to get him moving again. "I wonder what the lady from Georgia thought when they found these drawings. Or even the cowgirl?"

"Sorry. Not my area of expertise, unfortunately."

Maybe he wasn't such a stick-up-his-rear academic. He'd actually smiled and nearly laughed. She'd always been a sucker for a man who could laugh at the world and himself. Sort of like she was a sucker for a man in a kilt or out of it—whoa! He was a colleague and temporary lodger. She had to stop remembering brushing against him and the charge of something a little dark and a lot exciting. It had been a long time since she'd felt anything like that. Maybe never.

"Come on. You'll probably want to spend a while looking around, and I need to write up my report." She led Reese up the incline toward the drawings that decorated the wall just to the left of an overhang of red and dusty beige rock.

"Report?"

"I might be a 'civilian' but I am more than capable of providing the college with my assessment of the area."

He nodded, then asked, "Are there multiple locations with drawings and obvious signs of habitation?"

"This one is the closest to the ranch. There are more extensive ones a day's walk away. Others aren't in restricted areas, so I get to those in the ranch pickup or on horseback."

He looked away before he said, with a return to clinical stiffness, "My research focuses on the diet of late Bronze Age man—"

"And woman," she added because his tone hit her "annoy" button again—she'd thought she'd disconnected it after years in the corporate world. She needed to work on that, especially if she planned to return to a corporate job…eventually.

"And woman. Technically the Americas did not have a Bronze Age. There was no bronze until after the colonial period. I'm specifically interested in how legumes entered the diet here."

Jeez! Just when she'd thought he wasn't a pompous professor. "Hmm," she said, a noise that could mean anything.

"Pardon me. You're not a student and you probably know more about the area and its early inhabitants than I do."

Whoa, Nellie! Down, girl. Sure he'd just said she had intelligence and had apologized, but her only job was to act as hostess and not a hostess with benefits. If he wanted *that*, then he could drive himself to Nevada. Still in his utilitarian khakis—and she knew exactly what they were hiding—he had a certain charm.

JONES LOOKED UP the incline, not paying much attention to the flora, fauna or prehistoric graffiti. All he noticed was the very fine swing of the pixie's hips as she led her pixie-sized donkey. He should feel awkward, like a giant in her miniature world. Her car—a Mini Cooper—matched her undersize lifestyle. Instead, he got that same low-in-the-gut heat that had stirred when she'd brushed up against him that day with the scorpion. *Randy* came to mind to describe his state. He shook his head as he moved again. His brain certainly wasn't working at full capacity if he was coming up with Victorian descriptions of his state of…interest. He watched her more closely. Was that a natural swing? Or did she know that he was watching?

"Which group does the department at the university attribute these drawings to?" he asked as he drew close to her and the overhang that created a shallow cave-like space.

"They don't have a specific group but have dated the area's settlement to around 400 CE."

"Hmm." She proved to him again that she was more than a cute pixie-sized cowgirl. She was a woman with intelligence.

"The college recently received the property and hasn't funded any formal explorations, although the sites have been documented over the years." She dropped the donkey's lead rope. She pointed and said, "Right there, see?"

He moved up beside her, close enough to touch. The hairs on his arms stood at attention. He looked over her head to faint white markings just to the left of the shaded overhang, stepping around her and forward so his back was to her. He stared at the drawings, mentally going through the list of British kings, starting with Alfred the Great. By the time he got to Ethelred the Unready, he had everything under control and could look at her again. "What do they symbolize?" He pointed to a zigzag pattern.

She shrugged. "There's been a lot of speculation. Water or maybe wind or the deity for one of those elements. There are researchers who think that the glyphs are astrological, like Stonehenge."

He snorted. *Stonehenge.* He'd not get started on that. "Are there more?"

She nodded and moved into the shallow cave and the deep shadows. "It's cooler here, too. This is where I planned to stop for lunch. You explore. I'll get the packs from Reese."

Lavonda turned from him and wiped her palms down the sides of her jeans. Was she nervous? She didn't seem like the kind of woman who was squeamish about bugs or animals that might be hiding in dark places. She nearly tripped on the uneven rocks on her way to the animal. Then she stopped, straightened her back and easily took off the smaller cooler tied to the burro's saddle. That didn't seem very Wild West, as he'd imagined it when he was a boy. Maybe because they weren't in the Wild West. They had mobiles, satnav and sunscreen.

He turned back to the wall with its faint but still-visible drawings. He moved farther to the right and closer to the end of the overhang where a shallow indentation had been made by someone. How old was it and what had this been used for? His archaeologist's interest was piqued. He heard Lavonda talking to Reese. He walked slowly, not disturbing anything. Then he caught dull silver, glinting in the sunlight that barely reached under the overhang. A twenty-first-century drink can—or something older? He reached into his pocket for his mobile and the flashlight app. He shone it into the cave's dark corners.

"What did you find?" Lavonda's hushed voice whispered over his skin.

"Probably nothing, but I saw… Ah, just there." He pointed a little to the right and up on the wall.

Lavonda moved closer and a shiver of awareness skittered through him. Distracted for a moment, the flashlight beam swung wildly.

"Did you see something?" She touched his forearm briefly, her small fingers leaving a heated impression.

"Not yet," he said calmly, as if he was in a lecture hall and not standing next to an enchanted pixie, maybe a *leannán sí* who'd taken possession of his body like a succubus out of a Scottish fairy tale. He concentrated on the beam of light and what had caught his eye.

"There it is." Her arm shot out to point. She leaned in farther. Her breasts brushed against the outside of his arm.

It took all of his concentration to keep the light steady. "Yes." He made himself move closer to the glint and away from her warmth, carefully moving his feet to minimize any disturbance of the site. Habit. He needed that habit to keep his brain working. Otherwise, all he would think about was the pixie hovering by him, her darkly sweet scent of molasses and… oats? He looked over his shoulder and noticed the little donkey, his ears standing up and watching the two of them. "Your animal. Is he loose?"

"What?"

He gestured with his head, savoring again the brush of her light touch on his arm as she turned to deal with the animal. As he got closer to what he'd glimpsed, he saw exactly what had been reflecting the light. Another niche, this one definitely enlarged by a tool. He ran his fingers over the surface, noting the notches in the stone. The mica and pyrite in the stone had created the flashes of light. The blackened spots made it clear a candle or other light source had occupied the niche. That made sense with the reflective—

"Oh, that's amazing," Lavonda said, once again close.

"This cave has been used before."

"Oh, yeah. Any place that gives you shelter from the sun has been used. If not by the Tohono O'odham or Pascua Yaqui, then by ranchers, missionaries or animals. It's important to have shelter in the desert, even the high desert."

He nodded, lost in the crackling heat that surrounded her like the auras around the saint statues that filled every Arizona mission. Is that what the artists had been trying to portray? What was he thinking? This was not a divine feeling. This was the basest of urges. He stepped away from the raw, overwhelming urge that unbalanced him. "I'm sure the university has mapped and noted this location."

He'd traveled to Arizona to save his reputation and to finally be seen as his own man and not just the *younger* Kincaid brother. To do that, he needed to keep his distance from everyone, especially Lavonda. His secret could be discovered. He knew if she found out why he was really here, she would tell the college's president. She was just that kind of woman— honest, forthright…a cowgirl. Remain aloof, separate, he told himself. Otherwise, he might just talk himself out of his plan. It would be easy enough to forget what was waiting for him in Scotland if he took her into his arms, if he kissed her like there was no tomorrow, if he… If he did absolutely nothing, they would both be better off, so that was what he would do.

"What's for lunch?" he asked, turning from her and toward the sunshine slanting into the darkness, highlighting the miniature donkey whose head was buried in the open cooler. "I believe that Reese has beaten us to it."

Chapter Three

"Damn it, Reese," Lavonda said as she raced to the front of the cave, away from Jones and the crackling heat between her and the Scottish Clint Eastwood. "Get out of there. You don't like empanadas." She yanked the donkey's questing nose from the cooler she'd left open. What had she been thinking? Getting under Professor Kincaid's kilt, that's what. She dragged the donkey outside and into the shade thrown by the rocks, tying him to a small mesquite bush. "Stay here. I've got food and water for you."

"Will we need to return to the ranch?"

"The food is good. It's all wrapped up. Reese just gave it a good sniffing. You can keep exploring, and I'll tell you when I have our lunch ready."

Jones stared at her, his exact expression unclear in the shadows of his hat. He gave a quick nod and moved away, gone and out of her sight before she could say anything, not that she had anything to say. She turned to the little burro. "Reese, kilts aren't sexy, right? Plus, he's the 'strong, silent' type, which is not my type, right?"

The donkey's ear swiveled at the sound of her voice, but he kept his back to her. Obviously, he was miffed she'd kept him from destroying their empanadas. She pulled out the small bag of feed and the larger container of water, getting the donkey set up for his own lunch. He moved in on his food, and she patted his withers as he munched. "You know what Jessie would tell me?" she asked the donkey, changing her stance to mimic her long, tall cowgirl sister. "'Lavonda, don't go messin' with a man unless your intentions are clear.'"

Yeah, exactly what did that mean? She gave Reese a final pat and unpacked their human food. No matter what, she did owe the college and her friend Gwen to keep the visiting professor fed and safe. So far she hadn't done so well, nearly killing him with Cat and then the scorpion.

"Yo, Jones," she yelled out, going for asexual female pal. "Lunch is ready." She waited for a response. Nothing. Great. With her luck, he'd fallen, hit his head on a rock and was now in a coma. "Jones," she shouted again. No response. He'd gone out of the overhang and to the left. She walked that way, scanning the area for his hat—his lucky cowboy hat—and khakis. She needed to find him before he died from heatstroke or was attacked by marauding javelinas. She pulled her mind back to Jones. He couldn't have gone far, even if he was out of her line of sight. She scanned the area, then caught the sun glinting off his deep auburn hair, its ruddiness overlaid with a rich chestnut. He'd taken off his hat. He shouldn't have done that. Smartest dumb man in the desert today. Visitors like him just didn't understand the power of the sun. With the dry heat, sweat evaporated so quickly that you didn't even realize you were sweating.

"Hey," she yelled to catch his attention. He turned. She walked carefully over the large and awkwardly placed boulders that looked as if a giant child had scattered them like marbles. "Lunch is ready."

He waved at her again. She couldn't figure out if he was dismissing her or beckoning her closer. She kept moving. He crouched closer to something at his feet. She thought he was near the dry riverbed, which turned into a full-blown river during the summer monsoons. He'd probably spotted the pottery shards that had washed down over the centuries.

"Did you find something interesting?" she asked when she was close enough to catch the hint of moss and pine scent that somehow clung to him in the dusty desert heat.

"I believe this is one of the metates that you discussed, and more drawings."

She looked down at the round hole in the flat rock, near to the riverbed, obviously man-made or, more accurately, woman-made. "That's it. Can you imagine how much stone people ate with their grain? I mean that's how those holes were made, years and years of grinding corn and whatever else."

He nodded, and then his head moved up and she saw his eyes scan the horizon.

She started her own lecture. "This region was heavily settled at different times, not like the pueblos up at Montezuma Castle…you know, up at Camp Verde." He shook his head. "Doesn't matter. You're not looking for anything that old anyway. This area was heavily settled when Father Kino came through here building missions and churches. You should go see San Xavier, even though Kino didn't build that one."

He squinted cowboy-style into the open desert but didn't say anything.

She felt obligated to go on to fill in the strong-silent-type quiet. It's what she did when there was a lull in conversation. "It's a huge tourist attraction. The priest founded a string of missions, from Mexico over to Baja, California."

He stood and gestured for her to go first.

She looked at him without looking at him. Had she bored the pants off him? *If only. Dang it.* She went on to distract herself from the memory of him, her and nothing between them but a thin layer of cotton. "We became part of the US in 1854 with the Gadsden Purchase. Before that it was definitely claimed by Mexico… Spain. Actually, it was Hohokam land… You know all that."

When she saw he now had on his patient, professorial expression she was certain he used on particularly dull students, her babble dried up. "Here's our lunch. Empanadas—"

"Spanish pasties. They stole the idea from us."

He startled a laugh out of her and, without thinking, she touched his arm. Tingling awareness shot through her body. She seriously considered whether one of them should steal a kiss. His lips softened. He must have read that on her face because his green eyes darkened. She leaned in enough to capture his cool and dark moss scent. *Stop.* She subtly shifted her body away and his features moved back into something that was a mix of "aloof academic" and Clint Eastwood in *Two Mules for Sister Sara*—a classic, according to Daddy. She didn't want to start anything, even if he was interested, which was hard to know for sure. It just wasn't the time or place, right? She'd been at a crossroads and restless for months now. On the other hand, maybe going against her usual type would knock her out of her holding pattern and onto a new path. *Yep, keep telling yourself that, sister.* This could be a disaster of epic proportions.

"Here." She thrust an empanada at him. She picked up her own and sat three boulders away, near Reese. He was just about as good at conversation as the professor, anyway.

Two DAYS AFTER his hike in the desert, the image of Lavonda with the cartoon-princess eyes and luscious lips kept distracting him while he video-chatted with his colleagues in Glasgow. The chair had asked him three times if they needed to reschedule the call because Jones had missed key points in the presentation. The situation was ludicrous. He'd pulled it together enough to finish the call and tie up loose ends on a joint project. One or two more calls, a review of the material and the project would be complete.

He was sure he'd never have been invited to work on this paper after Dolly-Acropolis—or the "ancient" burial site created by a manufacturer of baby dolls, as it had been described by the papers. The university had insisted on publicity for his find. They'd called in the press, thinking, as he had, that he'd find a significant Viking site, not a doll dumping ground. The toys had been destroyed and hidden because they'd been made with illicit products during World War II.

The company could have been fined and shut down, so they buried the evidence.

The damned dolls were the reason—at least part of it—he had to keep his search for Kincaid's Cache secret. If it came to nothing, no one would know and it wouldn't play over and over again on YouTube, courtesy of the video shot on camera phones by student workers.

If he found the cache, though, the dolls would be forgotten and he'd be back on his way to the top of the department. His colleagues would also have to acknowledge that he'd not gotten his position because of his brother.

Jones gathered his laptop and overstuffed file folder for the short walk to the nondescript building that housed Stanley's office. The man was head of the history department for the university's Angel Crossing campus, and Jones hoped he would have another recommendation for a guide. He'd looked at his problem from all sides. He didn't have the time to find a guide on his own in an unfamiliar place. Plus, after going out into the desert with Lavonda, he realized that while he might stumble on something on his own, a guide familiar with the area could help him quickly eliminate dead ends.

He also wanted to confirm the teaching schedule he had agreed to for the remainder of the spring and the full summer semesters. The seminar on identification techniques would not meet every day. Plenty of time to do both sets of explorations.

Jones paused at Stanley's door. The professor was speaking with Dr. Gwen Hernandez. He recognized the president of the college from her picture on the website. He hesitated but Stanley said, "Jones, come in. How are you settling in at Hacienda Bunuelos?"

"Pardon?"

"The ranch," Dr. Hernandez said. "It's the traditional name of the ranch, although we will be renaming it to honor the very generous alum who donated the property to the university."

"Very comfortable now that we've sorted the cat problem."

"The cat problem?"

Jones had been keeping himself dosed with medication. The damned animal had decided that she was his personal exterminator. Today there had been a small lizard outside his bedroom door.

"Have you met our president?" Stanley asked. Jones shook his head and his colleague made the introductions before gesturing for Jones to sit. "Now. What did you need from me?"

"I am currently without a guide. The gentleman I contracted cannot provide his services—"

"Wait," Dr. Hernandez said. "I know I authorized reimbursement for the guide."

"You did and I paid him. Now he says that he cannot begin the job for another month, which is unacceptable. He also was reluctant to return the deposit, but I believe I convinced him otherwise."

"Well, hell," Dr. Hernandez said.

"That's why I've stopped by for new recommendations for a guide, Stanley."

Stanley and Gwen had a back-and-forth about the legalities. Since he was not familiar with the area or the university's systems, Jones didn't have anything to contribute. Finally, Gwen snapped her fingers and grinned. "I've got it. Lavonda."

"What about Lavonda?" Jones asked.

"She can guide you. She knows the area well and has plenty of desert experience. It will allow you to do the preliminary explorations. Perfect short-term solution."

"Lavonda?" He had been keeping her at arm's length, worried his housemate would figure out his trip wasn't about beans. She was much smarter than he'd assumed a cowgirl would be. Of course, he'd been picturing a cowgirl with big hair, sprayed-on trousers, and big—

"Absolutely."

"But she—"

"I know she doesn't look like a roughing-it camper, but believe me, she's tougher than she looks. That girl has a bronc riding champion buckle."

Jones still hadn't reconciled her rodeo riding with the pixie-sized woman with the sleek hair, polished nails and soft skin, but her boots looked well used. "I don't know that—"

"Let me call her." Gwen pulled a phone from her pocket. "Stanley can help you look for a professional guide, but this will get you out in the field right away." She stood and walked out as she spoke to Lavonda.

"Gwen is a problem solver," Stanley said. "I'll call around, but most guides are booked in advance."

Jones's stomach roiled with excitement, fear, anticipation—he had no idea with what. He and Lavonda alone in the desert could be a recipe for disaster or... Affairs happened at dig sites. He'd seen more than one start during the plotting of a Bronze

Age village. His current decision must be based on what was best for his career, not what might get him into Lavonda's sleeping bag.

"Is there a problem with this woman?" Stanley asked.

Jones pulled himself together. "I just didn't understand that she had trail skills."

Stanley shrugged his narrow shoulders. "If Gwen says she does, then she does. It's not that unusual for a cowgirl."

Gwen entered, smiling, "She'll do it, and she's the kind of price we need. Free."

"Free? I don't think that we can—"

"Don't worry. We've have worked out an agreement. She understands that it's a temporary thing until you find a real guide. Her words. Not mine. So, Dr. Kincaid, we have that little problem solved. This is working out well. Our students are very excited for your seminar. I didn't realize that beans were so popular. Got to go," she finished abruptly.

Jones shook her hand and tried to read the older woman's face. There was something there that he couldn't quite put his finger on. It was like finding a number of pottery shards and piecing them back together. You knew it was a pot but not its shape.

Jones made himself leave the office at a stroll, unconcerned and confident. What had he just committed himself to? Days on end with a sexy woman affiliated with the university from which he was attempting to hide his real mission. Having an affair with a cowgirl had not been on the map or his plan, even if it seemed as though the Fates were setting things up that way.

Chapter Four

Back in her old life, Lavonda had been fearless, telling *60 Minutes* they couldn't film on her company's property and pushing away Anderson Cooper's mic. But when Gwen called, she'd caved, saying yes to leading the kilted giant on his search for beans. The older woman had been Lavonda's first boss. She'd helped her find her footing in the corporate world, from what to wear to understanding the hierarchy of vice presidents. Giving in to one friend meant facing another. Lavonda would have to call Olympia to back out of helping at her and her attorney husband's ranch. Lavonda felt bad about letting her down and worse because she'd been ducking calls. She just wasn't up to defending herself from questions about why living at the university's run-down ranch as the "caretaker" was a good career move.

"Hi, Lavonda."

Darn her friend. Why had she answered? Lavonda had hoped to just leave a message. "How's it going?"

"You don't want to know. Remind me again why I thought it was a good idea to get married?" Olympia asked, her tone somewhere between exasperation and affection.

"Because it was easier than arguing with a lawyer about it?"

Olympia laughed. "You got that right. What's up?"

"The university roped me into helping out an archaeologist. I've got to babysit him while he wanders the desert, make sure that he doesn't die, that sort of thing. I'll be out on the trail for at least a week, and I might have to go out with him again later. I'm sorry but I won't be able to come to the ranch for a while."

"No problem. Cal's getting better at helping, and Spence's law practice is doing well enough that we've even hired someone to come out a couple of times a week to help around the place."

"That's good." Lavonda could see Olympia's stepson puffing out his chest as he did barn work. He'd been so sick as a little guy that any kind of "man's work" made him strut around proudly.

"What about you? Besides this guide thing, what else do you have going on?"

"I'm still doing work for the university when they need it." She knew her friends and even her family had begun to worry at her lack of focus. "I've got a couple of possible projects on the horizon."

"If you say so. What's he like? Egghead, right?"

"Why would you assume my guidee is a man?"

"Sorry. This person."

"It is a man. Scottish. He showed up in a kilt and everything."

"What? Wait. A kilt?"

"He competes in Highland games and agreed to be on the Angel Crossing campus team at an event in Tucson. Although why anyone would think Arizona was a good place to wear wool is beyond me."

"So he wears a kilt, does manly competitions and digs in the dirt?"

Lavonda ignored the implied question and went on, "He's studying beans, which apparently is an exciting thing if you're an archaeologist. Gwen is trying to talk me into writing press releases. Not sure how that's going to work, but I could be up for the challenge. I mean how do you make studying beans not the punch line to a fart joke?"

"The beans are definitely lowering his sexy level."

"What do you care about his sexy level?"

"I'm looking out for you. If you're not concentrating on finding a job, then you should be concentrating on your love life."

"Who decided you should be my own private dating service?" Lavonda did not want to think about the havoc Olympia and Lavonda's sister, Jessie, could wreak if they had any idea that Lavonda had looked at Professor McNerdy and imagined…things that should not be said to nosy sisters and friends.

"I didn't realize you were so touchy." Lavonda almost heard the shrug through the phone. "Anything else going on besides the hottie in the kilt?"

"He's not hot," Lavonda protested.

"I knew it. He's hot and you're interested."

"How could you know that?"

"Because I know you and now you've just admitted it. There's one good thing about being married to a lawyer—you learn all kinds of sneaky ways to get people to admit to things."

"That's not fair."

"You should have told me you were interested in this guy instead of pretending it was all business."

"But it is."

"I know your mama told you that lying is a sin."

"If—and that's a big if—anything goes on between the two of us, that's our business."

"Like what was going on between Spence and me was our business, right?"

"That was different. You were living together."

"Yep, that makes this so different."

"You were pregnant and there was Cal, too. A lot more was at stake."

"Don't try to wiggle out of this," Olympia said with the tone of no-nonsense authority that had crept into her voice since becoming a mother.

"Hey, don't go telling Jessie any of your fantasies about my love life. I don't need her sisterly advice."

Olympia laughed. "I won't need to tell her anything. As soon as you start talking about this guy, she'll know. What's his name anyway?"

"Jones."

"As in 'Indiana'?"

She smiled. Could the academic really be nicknamed for a movie character? "Could be. Wouldn't that be a hoot and a half."

The two women talked about what Lavonda would need for the weeklong hike, then Olympia said, "If you like this guy, go for it. Maybe it's just what you need."

"How about I just focus on keeping the two of us safe and sound in the desert. The poor man almost bit the big one when a scorpion crawled up his leg, but Cat saved him."

"Dang it. I wish I had time to hear that story, but Cal's bus will be here any minute."

"I'll tell you later."

Olympia was right. She couldn't deny that she was

attracted to Jones, despite his strong-silent-type swagger. Mama would call him a volcano under an ice cap. Although there was no reason she and Jones had to act on their mutual attraction. God, that sounded like corporate speak. Sure. An affair or fling might be fun and *might* even make her feel she was living rather than marking time. Except, in college she'd tried the just-sex thing. That hadn't ended so well. What if it wasn't just her lady parts that wanted Jones? Plus, the professor didn't live in the real world, really. He might not understand how a fling worked. She didn't want to hurt him, even if he could be a pompous jerk. Then, she could lose her job and the place that had begun to feel like home if she "fraternized" with the guest. Not that anyone had said anything, but Jones sort of, kind of, was her boss.

So the best approach was the one she'd been hanging on to: wait-and-see. Wait and see if she could figure out what to do next. But how much longer could she wait to get back in the game? The downsizing had made for a good break, time to recharge her batteries, plan her next move. Made her realize, being out here, how much she enjoyed ranch life. This was supposed to be a detour on her way back to an office with a view and a lot of zeroes after the first number on her paycheck. She'd guide the Scot, write a press release or two for Gwen and have one final cowgirl adventure before slipping back into her tailored wardrobe and heels.

"Excuse me."

Lavonda stood with her back to him, her head cocked to the side, the sunlight coming through the open barn door outlining her petite curves that hid a surprisingly hot strength.

"Yep," she said without turning to him. She ran her hands over the little donkey, her touch light but sure. Jones refused to let himself imagine those hands on him. He needed to have a conversation with her about their trip and his expectations. Business. Focus. His career and reputation were riding on this expedition.

He hadn't planned for a guide who might have the intelligence to figure out that what he was searching for wasn't what he said he was searching for. Plus, Dr. Hernandez had explained Lavonda would write stories about his explorations for the alumni magazine and even the local newspapers.

"I would like to go over our schedule for this first foray," he said clearly and precisely with a tinge of authority, like he did in a classroom full of students.

"Shoot," she said, not lifting her head but scooting around the donkey and bending over, her nicely compact and rounded bum facing him.

"I know that you were drafted into guiding me because of your familiarity with the region and as a favor to Dr. Hernandez. However, I have done extensive research and have a satnav to adequately direct us."

"Good. We won't be wandering around like Moses, then." She stood up and stepped away from the little animal, who stared at Jones with a hostile roll of his eye. "Anything else?" she asked, interrupting the staring contest between him and the burro.

"You have a confidentiality agreement with the university?"

Her eyes widened. "Sure."

"Are you certain? This is important because when I go into the field, I do not—"

"All right, hoss, let me tell you how it will be. I know that you're the boss of the search. But I'm the guide, which means I make sure you have food and water and you don't die out there."

"I doubt that's—"

"Do you want me to show you the stories? The desert isn't anything to fool with. I know it seems like we're close to civilization, that it's just a 'little warm' and whatever else you imagine. We're going out into rough terrain that may not get any signal, other than satellite—"

"Which I have."

"I studied the area you want to explore, and it isn't well mapped, even though it's relatively near to the ranch, because the things that draw any kind of settlement haven't changed that much over the years. Those things would be shelter and water. There is a very deep well here, and my guess is that a couple of the settlements nearby had small wells that probably ran out over the years and the groups moved on."

"Still, this is not something for which you've trained. Weekend and daylong treks notwithstanding."

"Excuse me?"

She blew air out of her nose and Reese shook his head while stamping a small hoof—a cartoonishly small hoof. Petite and pixieish, just like Lavonda. "Gwen wouldn't have suggested I take you out into the desert if I didn't know what I was doing."

"Were you a Girl Guide? Sorry. Um, a Girl Scout? Right? That's what they're called here."

She drew herself up to her fully unimpressive height, and he watched closely as her cheeks reddened with obvious anger. "First, I am a woman. Second, I have much more experience in desert survival than you. Third, I am saving your bacon, because while Gwen may not have said it, you would not have been permitted to go out exploring on your own."

"Saving my bacon?"

"You know, keeping this whole bean search from going south."

He knew what she was getting at. He knew exactly what happened when a project went "south," except this one at least wasn't being filmed. Never again. "Since I have done an exhaustive review of the literature as well as corresponding with local experts, I am certain that we will quickly and rather easily discover what I am looking for."

She looked down at Reese, whose ears drooped. The burro reminding him of a stuffed lop-eared rabbit he'd abandoned when his brother had teased him mercilessly.

She squared her shoulders and said, "I've led similar expeditions over the summers and breaks while I was in college. I have a fair amount of expertise… it just wasn't something that fit into my long-term plans in the end."

Whether he liked it or not, she was his guide if he wanted to get his search started sooner rather than later. Her familiarity with the area *could* help him locate the landmarks described in the journal, which had belonged to an ancestor who'd settled in the West at the turn of the last century. "I am sure that you are competent…more than competent."

"Whatever. It's temporary until the university finds you another guide."

"Again, I thank you for taking on this extra responsibility."

"You're welcome. Now, I'll make up a checklist for you." She led the burro back to his stall and strode from the barn. *Shite.* Why was he acting like a schoolboy by making her angry, when his very adult self wanted to watch her hips swing like that all day... and night?

LAVONDA STROLLED OFF with a nonchalance she worked on maintaining. Jones's comments had gotten way under her skin, which was silly. What did she care what a Scottish academic thought of her trail skills? It wasn't like she'd make a living out on the range. She'd decided long ago that ranching, horses and all that went with it weren't her future, after seeing the toll this lifestyle had taken on her sister—every time Jessie was thrown from a horse yet again or had fallen asleep during class after a weekend of rodeo competition. She and her family had worked so hard and had so little back then. Classmates had computers and Tony Lama boots. She loved the horses and didn't mind sweating, but she wanted the "riches" that should have followed all of that work. It didn't take much brainpower to figure out a job in an office with a big company might mean a lot of hours but also money for the computers and the boots.

So why did she feel like she had to prove herself to a wannabe cowboy, when she should be worrying about finding her next high-powered job?

Despite her annoyance with Jones, a tiny part of

her brain mulled over whether she could pull off accidentally forgetting to pack two tents so they'd have to share the one. What was wrong with her? She had never been the kind of woman—even as a teen—who made sex or men a priority. So had all of that stored-up sexual frustration exploded when Jones showed up in his kilt?

"Yee-owl," Cat protested on the back patio. She sat with her tail primly curled around her feet, but the narrowed eyes told another story.

"Cat, you've already had your food for the day. The vet has me under strict orders. He says that you've got at least six pounds to lose."

"Yee-owl."

"Sorry." Lavonda opened the door and Cat raced into Lavonda's quarters, entertaining the possibility she'd left a piece of kibble somewhere. As Lavonda created the list of items for Jones, she heard Cat's bowl being knocked around the small kitchenette. As she wrote, she peeked at Cat sitting by her empty bowl. The cat's tail did the slow twitch of annoyance. Lavonda leaned down and picked up the bowl quickly enough to miss the swat.

"Yee-owl."

"What is wrong with that animal?" Jones asked, appearing from nowhere outside her door—a good distance outside of her door. She jumped.

"You nearly gave me a heart attack." Dang it, that flutter in her heart had moved to points south.

"You said something about a list."

"I just printed it out. We'll go over it quickly. I'm sure you have the majority, if not all, of the equipment. As you pointed out, this is not your first rodeo."

"I'm certain I didn't use those exact words."

"Probably not, but close enough for government work."

He shook his head a little. "You're lucky that I watch American programs on television. Otherwise, it would be like you were speaking Greek."

"Indubitably, Jones, my man."

"Your knowledge comes from Masterpiece, right? All Americans watch that and think they know the British, although not so much the Scots."

"No Masterpiece for me. I'm more old-school. *Ab Fab* and *The Vicar of Dibley* and really old old-school, *Are You Being Served?*"

"No *Doctor Who* or *Agatha Christie*?"

"I like comedies."

"I see." He gave her a once-over and then turned away. "I don't think there's enough allergy medication for me to come in there with the cat. Who, by the way, can't keep her paws out of my Hobnobs."

"At least you're not sneezing. I'll meet you on the back patio. That way, if I'm contaminated by any cat hair it shouldn't kill you."

"I'M ALMOST BEGINNING to like this," Jones said, indicating the long, tall glass of amber liquid Lavonda had brought with her. "It has the look of Scotch. Maybe that's why?"

She couldn't stop herself from grinning just a little. "So no iced tea in the Highlands?"

"I do not live in the Highlands. But no, iced tea is not a beverage of choice. Hot tea is, of course."

"Of course. Drink up because we won't be having it on the trail."

Sitting at the rustic patio table, he scanned the list quickly. He asked for clarification on items and pulled a pen from somewhere to make checkmarks and notes. Their iced teas were empty by the time they'd gone through each point.

"We'll be using tents, not sleeping under the stars around the campfire?" Jones asked.

Lavonda felt the flush, remembering what she had been thinking about their sleeping arrangements. "Tents make sense for protecting equipment as well as people. It's early enough in the spring that nights are rather chilly."

"In Scotland, tents keep the rain off the equipment. I would guess that's not the problem here."

"Not usually. If we were going during monsoon season, that would be different."

"Monsoon season?"

"Summer storms come out of the Pacific and dump a ton of rain. Not that much of it sticks around. The ground is so hard it pretty much just runs off. Arizona is not known for its gentle rains."

"No smirr."

"Smirr?"

"Mist, drizzle. Typical Scots weather."

"It's totally different in the winter. In Phoenix the pollution just lies in a haze with no wind or storms to blow it through."

"You've lived here your entire life, right?" Jones had leaned back in his chair.

"Not here, but in Arizona, when we weren't on the road with the rodeo. Though my mama is from Texas. Daddy's people hail from Arizona."

He grinned at her. "Your accent changed when

you talked about your parents. Do they live nearby? Any siblings?"

Her cheeks heated in embarrassment. But then, why should she be all hot and bothered about going a little country? "My parents are near enough, by Arizona standards. I have a younger brother who lives in Angel Crossing. My sister has a place outside Phoenix. What about you?"

"My brother is older and a professor at the university, too."

"Your parents?"

"My father is retired from the same university and Mother gardens."

"In a castle?" she asked, just to get a rise out of him. It worked.

"That's our summer home."

She grinned. "It's good that you're all close."

"Not that close," he said in a tone that told her they were at the end of this line of discussion.

She decided to not take the hint. "So you always wanted to be an archaeologist? Sounds like a family tradition. Since your brother's in the same field."

The emotions that raced across his face moved so quickly she'd barely understood them before they were hidden behind his usual mask of flat professional detachment. She'd seen, though, a soul-deep hurt.

"We had standing stones at the edge of our property. Iain and I set up a dig. We'd seen a program about it on television. I found a bead and a pottery shard. He found a jawbone, and we were hooked. We set up digs every summer with our friends. The biggest find was a Roman coin that I sold for a hundred quid. We split it four ways and bought sweets. And I purchased a trowel because my mother complained about us using hers. She would sometimes make us stop our work so she could get back her tools."

"I bet you still have that first trowel." She delighted in watching him fidget with discomfort. She shouldn't be encouraging him to dig at his childhood, because it made him a little too endearingly cute.

"Yes, well, my parents were tolerant to a point. My mother had hoped one of us would follow in her grandfather's footsteps and become a solicitor, but Iain and I were stuck on archaeology."

"Is that how you got the nickname?"

Darn it. Now a cute-as-a-button blush lit up his high cheekbones, highlighting the smattering of freckles.

"I did a school project where I explained why the archaeology of the Indiana Jones movies was inaccurate. The name stuck. But your history is much more fascinating than mine. You won championships?"

Now she shifted and looked away. Dang internet. "That was when I was a teen, and I didn't have a lot of competition. It was our family business, though none of us are still in it. There weren't too many girls riding broncs—not like the guys—though the bull riders get all of the attention now. Jessie, my sister, rodeoed for a number of years, but she's got her riding rehab program now."

"That's where Reese may go, right?" he said, the cool facade slipping. She could see the eager student he must have been and the focused academic he'd become. He smiled encouragement for her to go on, and Lavonda couldn't resist. She explained how the burro would fit into the therapeutic riding program Jessie had started for children with physical and mental challenges. The iced-tea pitcher was empty by the time Lavonda noticed the setting sun. "It's getting late. I have a lot to prepare before we leave."

They stood. She hesitated, feeling that maybe she should offer to make a meal. It had been part of the contract, although he hadn't insisted she cook for him. Probably best for all involved, especially his stomach. Her relief had nothing to do with the intimacy of sharing a meal, she insisted to herself.

"Yes. I must look for my protection."

Her heart stopped for a moment. What the hell was he saying? She choked out, "I don't think that will be necessary. I mean we'll each have our own tent. I wasn't imagining—"

"For my equipment."

She couldn't stop her gaze from going directly to his crotch. Horrified, she looked up quickly and caught the dark interest in his intensely green eyes. "It would be bad to get sand in—"

"In such sensitive…um…apparatus?"

"Absolutely," she answered, her heart beating fast. "The heat and sun can do damage to the gear, too."

"I wasn't expecting it to be a daytime affair, but if you insist," he said, a knowing smile curving just the corner of his lips.

"Now you're teasing."

"Maybe. Lavonda…don't you think we should get all of this out of our system before we're all alone in the desert?"

"Get all what out of your system? I'm the guide. You're the guidee."

"Let me show you." He stepped forward much quicker than a man of his size should be able to move, pulled her to him and curl-the-toes kissed her.

Chapter Five

Jones refused to analyze beyond the obvious why he was kissing Lavonda. He nibbled at her soft mouth, slipping his tongue in to taste the earthy spice that would remain forever tangled up with his memories of the dry desert heat. He pulled her closer. Her hands moved to rest on his jaw before stroking down his neck in a barely there touch that made him shiver.

"Should I show you more?" he asked, moving his lips to her cheek, while wanting to bury his face in her neck. To slow down his pulse, he placed his hands on her shoulders, feeling the delicate roundness.

"We can't. I don't think…"

"No thinking." He whispered across her lips. She didn't pull back. He went in for another kiss, another nibble, another taste. She opened her mouth, her tongue sweeping in and tasting him right back, connecting directly to his groin. He needed to stop before they went further. He'd not been thinking when he started this, but he needed to engage his brain now. To prove that this was something they could control. Or, at least, *he* could control, so when they were alone he'd be able to concentrate on what was important and not the lush softness of her lips.

He made himself step back and turn from her. "I'll check the list," he said, getting his breathing under control. "I'll be ready to head out day after tomorrow."

He walked as calmly as he could from the patio and into the house, his control tattered. Not a good thing when he was here to repair his reputation. Getting close to her would make it more likely that she—and, therefore, both universities—would discover his lie.

He sneezed. Damn it. The cat had contaminated the whole house. He focused on his current misery to get himself back under control. He'd used a ruthless self-discipline to barrel through university and up the academic ladder. Now he needed to call on his focus to put Lavonda and the kiss out of his mind.

Or he could make an argument that a brief affair with Lavonda would be okay, the sort of thing that happened in the field. Who would know? They would be in the desert on their own. He'd be back in Glasgow by fall and never see her again. Perhaps she wouldn't guess what his true purpose here was. Perhaps there was no need to dismiss her or her lips so quickly. He sneezed again.

All right. First things first. Another dose of medicine, then a trip to the shops for whatever he needed from the list, including the protection she probably hadn't listed but he was beginning to think he'd better pack. Suddenly, the daunting task of finding his ancestor's secret cache and keeping it under wraps while not succumbing to his allergies no longer seemed like too much of a problem.

"YOU'VE CHECKED YOUR PACK?" Lavonda asked Jones in the early-morning chill. "We can't come back for anything you've forgotten."

"I'm not a novice," he answered formally, because he'd reminded her of that more than once. His guide had changed from the sexy pixie into a frowning, impatient perfectionist.

"Let's go, Reese," she said to the burro, who was laden with a goodly portion of the equipment. The remainder was split evenly between his horse and hers. Jones put on his sunglasses and gestured for her to move in front of him. Reese dropped his head and ears, a forlorn figure.

An hour into the ride, Jones had warmed sufficiently to strip off his jacket. He lifted his camera to take a shot of the landscape. And by landscape, he meant the rear aspect of his guide. She turned suddenly, and he moved the lens to the surrounding countryside. Damn. He'd evolved years ago from a horny sixteen-year-old ogling girls. Though he still remembered how superior he'd felt when the perfect Iain had been caught taking snaps of girls at a topless beach they'd snuck onto during a holiday trip— using the new camera his parents had given him for achieving perfect marks.

"Do you think that outcropping ahead might be the one you're looking for?" Lavonda pointed to an arrangement of rocks and boulders that provided a natural shelter. She was thinking about it as a possible native settlement for his cover expedition. But based on the coded journals, he thought it *might* be one of the trail markers.

Keep his real search a secret, find the cave, save

his career and redeem his reputation. This was going to be difficult. His ancestor had come to the Americas for similar reasons, and if the journals could be believed—if Jones had properly decoded the entries—then that Kincaid had discovered a cave full of ancient relics. He needed to—

"So? Stop or move on?" Lavonda asked, turning to him, sipping water.

He squinted at the overhang to appear that he was seriously considering it. His horse, Joe, shifted under him impatiently. The formation wasn't quite right. He needed to find one that looked like a woman's breast and to the right would be an arched cat. He couldn't tell her that, though, because he was supposed to be looking for ancient settlements based on previous scholars' research, which included coordinates, not lewd descriptions.

"Let's move closer and see if there is anything there," she said before he could respond, urging her gelding through the scrub and rock. She moved easily with the shifting gait of the dun-colored horse, its black tail switching lazily. She fit both the saddle and the desert somehow, her small stature not overwhelmed by the big-footed horse, cacti and craggy mountains.

He followed her more slowly to gather his thoughts. What might make a credible explanation for why this wasn't a location to explore? When he caught up with her and dismounted, the overhang, thankfully, looked even less promising as the location for even a temporary settlement. "I don't know," he said slowly, as if this had possible significance. He moved around to examine the space from different angles. He straight-

ened with finality, hands on his hips, thinking he'd
spent an appropriate amount of time in his exami-
nation.

"Anything that might have been here is probably
gone," she said, and pointed to the bare rock path.
"There have been a lot of washouts here." She looked
toward the slopes of the mountains that were still distant. "This looks like the beginnings of an arroyo.
And look here—you can see where these boulders
have moved. That kind of scarring has to be recent
or it wouldn't be visible."

He nodded because everything that she'd noticed
made sense. "We'll look elsewhere, as this is rather
distant from the coordinates of the previous finds."
What a pompous ass he sounded.

She nodded, paused for just a second before easily
getting herself into the saddle, and looked at both him
and his horse with a professional courtesy. "I know
that you have a survey of the area. Maybe you should
be leading. You know what you're looking for."

If she only knew. This was more complicated than
he wanted. Of course, he'd planned to have a guide
who could have cared less what he was doing as long
as he got paid. He had to take a chance and use the information he'd gleaned from the diaries. He could tell
her...a colleague had recently sent him new research?
Would she believe that? He could say the colleague
had sent references to an old text that indicated the
locales, but the exact locations had not been plotted
yet. That might work. In fact, it was near enough to
the truth that he might pull it off.

"Are there any specific land formations I should

be on the lookout for as we near the coordinates?" she asked.

Finally, something on this godforsaken trip was going his way. She'd given him the opening he needed. "Just before we set off, I received research from a colleague that is based on an old source... the journal of a European explorer." He deliberately slowed his speech, acting like a professor allowing note-taking students to catch up. "He...this explorer mentioned unique rock formations my colleague had not had the opportunity to map."

"Hmm... I'm not sure if that will help. They could have changed and there's a lot of desert. Were any settlements noted? We have a pretty good listing of those—depending on the year. We should be able to get a good enough signal to pull something up on the GPS."

Jones dug into his rucksack for his tablet to give himself a little more time to refine his story. "In addition to the landmarks, this explorer did give locations based on settlements. One of them was the Los Santos Angeles de Guevavi mission."

"That's good. That hasn't moved."

"The trouble may be that from that locale he makes note of rock formations and we are not starting from the mission."

"That's where I come in. I've got my handy-dandy phone. I can pull up a satellite map and work backward. I bet between both of us, we can locate the settlement. The mission is just a ruin, though, not open to the public. If we need to go there, I'll let Gwen know what we're doing and there shouldn't be any trouble."

Possibly having a smart guide wasn't all bad. Other than she might find him out and being clever made her even hotter. He turned slightly away and said, "I'll need to search through my notes for the exact details."

"Hey, it's near enough to lunch. Let's go just a little farther to that overhang up ahead." She pointed to another rock formation that had an enticing patch of shade created by a cantilevered slab of rock, not that different from the one they'd explored on her trip to check the metates and petroglyphs. When they finally stopped and she dug out the meal, he barely tasted it as he searched for anything he could use to narrow down the location. The two of them discussed the noted landmarks in reference to their current trek.

"From his descriptions and looking at the map, I'd say it's east of here, probably by ten miles or so."

"Why?" he asked, but kept his eyes on the materials on the tablet. Her proximity wasn't as distracting if he didn't look at her.

"It's the arroyo he describes in his notes. I know he didn't call it that, but it certainly sounds like an arroyo. I found one like that. It may have changed since his time, but there is a large flat rock with five metates in a circle. It's weird. Usually, metates aren't spaced like that. Old explorers imagined that they were all sorts of things."

"That could be what he talks about as the pentagram. Lead on. You are the guide, after all."

"For now. But you're the expert."

"Expert on beans. You know the land. Shall we try that direction?"

"All right. Let's pack up and go. You ready, Reese?" she said to the burro, who had been eyeing their food.

"Lunch meat gives you gas, and none of us wants that."

Her comment startled a laugh out of Jones.

"What?"

"I don't know…it's just—"

"Women in Scotland don't talk about farts?" She grinned.

"Not that I've noticed."

"You mustn't be hanging out with the right crowd. Or with women raised with a brother who was overly fascinated by all bodily functions, the grosser the better."

Why did such a childish conversation make him feel happy? Because he was a pathetic git. "You're probably right."

"We'll camp when we get to the arroyo. It'll be near the end of the day anyway and then we can explore the area thoroughly tomorrow." She efficiently packed up the meal and didn't wait to see if he followed.

Camping tonight. One tent or two? Which way did he hope they'd go?

Soon he'd be back in Scotland after a successful search. Then he could restart his life and finally get out from under his brother's shadow. With the discovery of Kincaid's Cache, Jones would be able to get his career back on track. He could focus his research on the tales from the West, just as he'd always dreamed. That wasn't the "real" archaeology his brother and father insisted upon. But now he had a chance to prove himself. There was archaeology worthy of his study here and all over the West and tall tales, like the one from his ancestor, often had a basis in fact.

"WE'LL STOP THERE," Lavonda said, pointing to an open area surrounding large piles of boulders. He didn't even grunt in reply. He'd been somber since their lunch stop, not that she'd expected chatter on a ride.

"Fine." He rolled his impressive shoulders under his light khaki shirt. Joe lowered his head, obviously ready for a stop, too. "I bow to your superior trail knowledge."

Was that a backhanded compliment? Or just a snarky comment? She ignored it, just like she did her brother when he was in a mood. She couldn't put off deciding about the tent situation. She'd packed two, but could set up just one of them. After that kiss… Was she really a fling kind of woman? She'd do another kick the can down the road on this decision, too. Yes, until the sun went down, at least. Why hadn't she packed tequila or at least a couple of bottles of wine? Because this was not a pleasure trip. Remembering that made it clear to her that she'd be setting up two tents.

Reese brayed and shook himself, making his pack lurch. He trotted forward to the area she'd planned for camping. The donkey had a sixth sense about water and good camping spots, according to the former caretakers.

She needed to set her mind firmly on business. Because that man was temptation, like seven-layer lemon chiffon temptation. Reese continued to trot, slowing to a lope when she and her horse were within ten feet of him, then rushing forward. The little donkey bypassed the space by the dry riverbed she'd planned for their stop, instead scrambling up the hillside to a shallow cave that sheltered a flat space large enough for two tents and a fire. She wasn't sure she should believe in the burro's alleged talents. The sky looked stormy, too, but the weather was far-off. Still, the darned animal might be right. Finding higher ground was a better-safe-than-sorry bet. A dry riverbed could fill up fast. Brownie, her very placid horse, had begun to look nervously at the sky.

"He's very nearly mountain goat, isn't he?" Jones said when he and his mount caught up.

"Burros are sure-footed. That's why they were so popular with miners. You should see them in the Grand Canyon. They're everywhere and never make a misstep." *Stop babbling, Lavonda. Set up camp with two tents.*

"Why didn't we stop at that sandy area?"

"That's a dry riverbed, and it looks like rain over there," she said, unpacking Reese and pointing with her chin. The storm was moving more quickly than she'd expected. She could dimly see the black sheets of rain, and it was getting dark fast.

"Can I help?" He stepped to her. Instead of the approaching storm, she could only catch Jones's pine-and-moss scent.

"Um…sure. Get the horses staked, unsaddled and settled," she said over her shoulder, moving equipment quickly so she could start on the tents. She'd get one up and put in all of the items that needed to stay dry. Then she'd work on getting the second one set up. Reese twitched against his lead line again. She knew how he felt. The storm was barreling down on them. Fortunately, Jones had cared for horses before. Together, they worked with minimal talking. They were ready to get the second tent up when the rain hit. Reese and his horsey companions found shelter against the rocks, butts facing the driving downpour. She sped into the tent, which was packed with equipment and filled with Jones's presence. Lucky she was small, because otherwise there wouldn't have been room.

Rain pelted the tent and lightning cracked. "Just in time," Lavonda said. "These storms don't last long, but they're intense while they're going on." In the illumination of the lightning, she saw him nod. "Is the lantern nearby?"

The tent filled with light. She scanned the space. All the important equipment looked to be here. Including both sleeping bags. "In that pack on your right are energy bars, if you need something to tide you over. There's water, too. Although lucky for us, I thought to put out other pans to catch the rainwater. Out here you never miss a chance to get more water."

"Hmm," Jones mumbled. He had an energy bar shoved in his mouth.

She laughed. "You should have said that you were starving. I could have gotten to the bars earlier."

"Didn't realize it until we stopped moving." He pushed the rest of the bar into his mouth, took a few manly chews, then swallowed.

"Better?" she asked. He nodded and then she saw him reach for water. That was good idea for both of them. The rain continued to fall hard, but the thunder sounded farther off. Probably another five or ten minutes and the storm would blow over. "Could you pass me some water, too?" He took a swig from the bottle, wiped off the top and handed it to her. She looked at the bottle for a moment before taking it. Why did sharing the bottle seem more intimate than kissing? She drank and decided that, like two tents, from now on there would be two bottles, because she could swear that she tasted him.

"Sometimes storms come up like this in Scotland."

"This one sounds like it might be slowing. It's unusual for this time of year. Most of our storms come in the summer—monsoons out of the Pacific."

The conversation dribbled to a stop. The glow of the lantern threw large shadows in the corner of the tent. Jones filled up more than the physical space of his body, though that was impressive enough. She'd been around large, strong men her whole life with Mama and Daddy on the rodeo circuit, but none of them had made her feel as small and helpless…feminine as Jones. Even the freckles that she noticed across the tops of his high cheekbones didn't make him seem less intimidating and masculine. He definitely wasn't the sort of man she should sleep with, right? Where was smart, logical Lavonda when she was needed? Because that gal would understand why it was such a bad idea to even "just" sleep with Jones. She would know that this would not end well, no matter what the other wild-for-action Lavonda had suggested at the beginning of this trip.

JONES KEPT HIS GAZE glued on his hands, knowing no matter what he did, it mustn't show how much he wanted her. He watched the shadows dance over Lavonda's curving softness, thinking he should say something to break the silence but not what he wanted to: *Come closer so I can kiss that soft spot behind your ear and let's see what happens next.*

"The big problem out here is the ground," she said, startling him. He'd moved on to concentrating on not noticing her pleasantly earthy scent now that he wasn't watching her. She went on, "It's so dry that the sand and dirt get packed down like cement."

"Concrete," he said. "Cement is the ingredient. Concrete is the product." He could feel her glare. Good. That broke the tension.

"No matter what you call a cat, don't call it late for dinner. It means that the water—"

"That doesn't make sense. Is that an American saying?"

"Just something Mama says. It means that what you call it really doesn't matter because you understood what I was saying."

He harrumphed. Dear Lord. When had he transformed from caber-tossing Highland marauder into stodgy old professor? About the thousandth time he'd watched the Dolly-Acropolis video and promised himself that he wouldn't be lured by an impossible-to-ignore archaeological white whale. So what was he doing in the American desert if not being lured by a story…and a sexy cowgirl—a recurring fantasy from his teenage years?

"The water just runs off," she continued. The rain had stopped. "That means dry riverbeds are suddenly rivers. Worse. It might not even be raining where you are, but it rained at a higher elevation and suddenly there is a wall of water rushing down the arroyo."

"Sounds like you've had experience with that."

"Not me. But it's something that Mama and Daddy

taught us. They'd seen horses and cattle washed away. You don't fool around with that."

"You lived on a ranch?"

"Not really. We did rodeo. Daddy managed a place for a bit. We moved around before we settled in Arizona."

"The Kincaids have lived on the same lands for five hundred years." He could look at her again, his heart having settled back into a regular, slow rhythm.

"We lived in a trailer when I was growing up. Made it easy to move along. Mama said that there must be Gypsy blood in the Leigh family. They still travel a lot. Jessie and Danny are settled, though," she said wistfully, and he wanted to hear more. But she went on, "The rain is done. I'll get supper ready. I'm sure the energy bar won't hold you very long."

"It'll do." A few splatters of rain hit the tent. "Do you think others have ever sheltered under here?" he asked. The air in the tent suddenly got richer with her scent. A subtle heat radiated from her body. She shifted and another wave of her heady scent wafted to him.

"Possibly. This area has been home to a number of groups."

Thunder cracked so sharply the rocks seemed to shift. Lavonda's hand shot out as if to steady herself. He clutched it and then tugged gently so that she fell forward against his body. He didn't ignore what fate was presenting him, finding her lips for a quick, hard kiss that softened into something gentle. Like the rain coming down again just beyond the ledge. She allowed him to explore her mouth for a moment before her hands crept up his back and her fingers pushed through his hair. The feel of her small, strong fingers soothed and heated him. Her tongue touched his and he pulled her closer.

Jones didn't stop a deep hum of pleasure. Her hands moved to massage his neck, her mouth opening for him in a way that made it clear she wanted more. He pulled her upward so he had a better angle on her sweetly wicked mouth. He didn't even jerk as the next rumble of thunder vibrated through the rocks. Hadn't the storm been moving away? Then he stopped caring what the thunder, lightning and rain were doing, because this fierce woman was discovering his body with a thoroughness that made him gasp.

Lavonda shifted closer and he took that as encouragement to touch her. His hands moved surely, instinctively until he heard her gasp and moan.

"Yes. That. Do that again," she whispered against his mouth, trying to get even closer, moving her legs so that they fit around him, belly to belly.

"Here," he said, the *r* rolled into a growling noise he didn't recognize as his own voice.

Her head fell back in obvious delight and need. His mouth latched on to her neck and he scraped his cheek along the sensitive skin until she shivered in gasping pleasure.

"Lavonda," he whispered.

"Why can't it have an *r*?"

"What?" he asked, his lips moving from her.

She looked up and saw his eyes darkened to nearly black by his dilated pupils. Good God, she wanted him. "Nothing." She reached up and pulled his mouth back to hers. She tasted him, seeming to want to absorb the essence of him. His tongue swept her mouth.

Jones didn't care if she sounded crazy because she tasted perfect. She fit his arms perfectly. He wanted her and that was something he'd missed for months, maybe years. That wasn't right… Her moan focused his attention back to her, her taste a smoky hint of chili with the bright lightness of a fresh leaf. That was the high desert. He was home. He grabbed her tight, needing to feel those compact but feminine curves against him, melting into him.

"Wait," she said, leaning away from him for a moment. "What are we doing here?"

He didn't have enough blood in his brain to say anything but the truth. "We're going to get into that sleeping bag and I'm going to have my way with you."

"Oh." She exhaled. "Just so we're clear, but I don't have any—"

"I've got…" The words stuck in his throat because she had just unbuttoned her shirt. She wiggled to get out of his lap, but he couldn't resist touching his lips to the soft skin of her breasts not covered by her satiny bra.

Lavonda inhaled sharply but didn't stop moving until she had him pulled on top of her in the nest of sleeping bags. They fit together so well. His hand on her breast, her leg thrown over his hip so that their bodies aligned. His mouth stayed on her mouth even as she arched into him. She yanked at his shirt. He returned the favor by pulling off her remaining clothes. Next time—yes, absolutely next time—he'd take his time to explore every inch of her. He cradled himself between her thighs. She pushed lightly at his shoulder.

"What about—"

"I'm covered. No more talking. No more—"

She shut him up with her mouth and shifted. He knew just what she wanted from him. He took care of their protection then obliged her by moving into her surely, firmly. She sighed in pleasure and joy. For a moment they stayed like that, connected. The stillness stretching out until she lifted her hips just a little. He plunged into her, rocking with her again and again, forever. When she thought she couldn't reach any higher, she tightened and then shivered with pure and perfect delight. He growled out his pleasure and shuddered into stillness.

His heavy weight was pressing her into the ground. He rolled onto his back, where she naturally cuddled into his chest, her head fitting easily under his chin, his arm around her. He savored the last vibrations of her pleasure as he dozed off, pulling her a fraction of an inch tighter against him.

Chapter Six

Oh, crap. Lavonda had known even as she'd ached from Jones's touch that giving in was a bad idea. Now they'd done it. This was going to get awkward. Snuggled against his warmth, she felt his relaxed but still-solid muscles. Good. He was asleep. She squirmed away and found her magically disappearing clothing. Thank goodness, the rain had stopped. She quietly got out of the tent and took a long, deep breath.

Don't dwell on your mistakes or they'll build you a dwelling. Another gem from Mama. Repeating this one allowed Lavonda to focus on dinner rather than what had happened six feet away. She'd get the remainder of the camp set up on her own. The less sensitive equipment and supplies had been covered with the canvas of the other tent. As soon as she made sure Reese and the horses had come through the storm okay, she'd set up the other tent. They'd each sleep in their own quarters. Not that she wouldn't want a repeat of… No. She couldn't think that way. They were colleagues. Professionals. He wasn't staying, so maybe it'd be okay. They wouldn't have to work together forever, just until he flew back home. Of course, that all depended on whether Jones wanted a repeat.

"What's your opinion, Reese?" she asked as she came up to the little burro standing patiently at the edge of the overhang. His rear was only a bit damp. "No wisdom from the animal kingdom. I bet if Cat were here, she'd give her opinion." Reese looked over his shoulder at her in disgust. "You're just interested in food, none of this philosophy, right?" She stroked the donkey's head and gave him a pat before moving to the provisions to find his and the horses' feed.

Triple crap. The canvas hadn't been well secured and the supplies were drenched. Which wouldn't have been a disaster because everything was in waterproof containers, except—and she gave the donkey a long glare—a number of the food packages had been torn open and were ruined.

"Reese, you don't even like this stuff," she accused. She'd packed extra, but they'd still need to cut the trip short. "Thanks for making me look incompetent." Reese did not look regretful or interested.

Partway through separating the damaged from the still-sealed food, a scuffing and tiny bray from Reese told her that Jones had emerged from the tent. She knew her ears were red with embarrassment—good thing her hair covered them. She kept her head down and her gaze on the packets of food.

Jones cleared his throat. "Is there anything I can do to help?"

Her impulse was to tell him no. To tell him that she didn't need his help. That she was a big girl who could take care of herself and the camp without breaking a sweat. She needed to remember that she wasn't in the corporate world where she had to fight for every inch of respect and that a good cowgirl knew when to ask for a hand. "The other tent needs to be set up, and we have to check on the bedding. If it got wet, lay it out to dry."

"Is there anything left to eat?" he asked.

She smiled to herself. "Enough, but we'll need to head back to the ranch sooner than we planned. I packed extra but not that much extra."

"Did the animal do that?" he asked, close enough that she caught the whiff of pine and moss. The heat left her ears and headed south.

"Reese can't be trusted around food, apparently," she said, gathering herself to stay unconcerned by his nearness.

"Is the rain done?"

"Should be. Monsoons come in quickly and blow right back out."

"Scottish storms do that sometimes but we're more likely to get all-day rain. I wonder what—" He abruptly stopped.

"What?" she asked.

"Nothing."

Now she was curious. "Come on. What? How the prehistoric beans survived this kind of rain?"

"THAT'S IT." Every muscle in Jones's body tightened painfully as he realized he'd been about to spill the beans—another American expression that had nothing to do with his research. Could he blame the after-effects of what they had done in the tent? What he'd woken up wanting to do again?

The silence stretched out and grew tense as his

brain considered and discarded what he should say. Wouldn't she figure out what he was doing soon enough? Maybe not. He couldn't imagine that they'd find anything this trip.

"I had a relative, a distant cousin, who was an archaeologist and did explorations in Arizona." Completely true.

"Really? What part? Did he find anything? When was this?"

His heart beat a little faster. He was skirting so close to the edge of disaster. "He did find unusual items, just before the Great War... World War I." Now Kincaid's Cache was barely known. Would she find the nearly ancient history in terms of the Western US of any interest? She was a cowgirl, so maybe.

"Are they in any museums?"

"Not that I know of. I believe he may have sold what he found to fund his search," he said, and looked away.

"Too bad." She dug into a pack, then said, "So this archaeology is in your blood, huh? Any famous ancestors or finds?"

"No famous Kincaids, even the one who lived here. My search wouldn't have been noticed by anyone if that student hadn't uploaded his video." He stopped talking right then. She didn't know about Dolly-Acropolis and he wouldn't be the one to tell her anytime soon. "Not that many people saw the video." Except every archaeologist.

"You're on YouTube?"

"Isn't everyone? Nothing interesting, really." He needed to make sure she didn't look this up. "I'd been asked by the university to lead a project, based on documents that had been donated to the archaeology department. I had authenticated everything." Dear Lord. It did sound a bit like what he was doing now. "We all got a bit caught up in the promise of the materials." This story didn't make him sound any less like an idiot, as his brother had pointed out at the time. Iain was good at that sort of helpful suggestion. *Maybe next time you'll remember that you're an academic and not Indiana Jones,* he'd told Jones when he'd called after the heap of moldy dolls and not the pile of Viking-era artifacts had been shown and reshown on every news program. Also, after Iain had been named to the chairmanship that Jones had been promised.

"I'm guessing by that you didn't find anything?"

"The university is still arguing with the family who provided the documentation about whether someone ransacked the site and then hid or sold the artifacts."

"That must have sucked," she said with straightforward sympathy. Now he felt even worse.

He opened his mouth to say…something. Closed it again so he wouldn't have to lie any more today.

"Let's salvage what we can. Even though I brought extra food, I forgot that a man as big as you would need a lot of fuel." She smiled broadly. "Or that Reese would be so insistent on getting into the stores. If we're lucky and we're careful, we may only need to trim off one day."

"A reasonable plan." He reached out and touched her arm, going on the instinct he usually ignored and tugging her toward him. He needed her and soon enough she might not be speaking with him. She started to open her mouth, so he took full advantage, pressing their lips together to interrupt what she had to say. He finished the kiss and looked at her. Her long lashes lay against her cheeks and her chest jerked with her uneven breaths.

"Don't think you can just kiss me, and I'll do whatever you want." She glared up at him.

"No, ma'am," he said in what he hoped was a good imitation of a cowboy drawl.

Her sudden laughter made Reese bray in response. "Stick to digging up moldy jewelry, doc."

Her teasing didn't make him want to hide. Instead, he thickened his burr until he sounded like a caricature of a Scotsman. "Lassie, you'll appreciate my treasure-hunting skills later tonight."

Her eyes went a little hazy and she licked her lips. Now all he'd be able to think about as they made camp was what they'd be doing in that single tent later.

LAVONDA SCOOTED OUT of their shelter before the sun rose, leaving behind the solid warmth of Jones's arms. It wasn't exactly that she was upset by what they'd done. They were both adults and consenting. Nothing wrong with enjoying themselves, no matter her list of reasons to resist. The real trouble had been when her mushy, girly brain imagined a life with him, beyond the night. She couldn't go there.

"Okay, Reese," she said in a low voice as the burro smacked his lips and showed his teeth. "I'm getting you breakfast." His two companions stamped their hooves in agreement.

She looked up at the sky, which was uncharacteristically gray. Had the giant Scotsman brought his own weather with him? She shook her head at her own fanciful thoughts. Being out in the desert with the real world far away could make a person forget her reality: more or less unemployed with a long-term plan that had a lot of holes.

Well, she couldn't solve her future this morning, so she may as well focus on what she could solve. Find the best way to the arroyo and figure out how long their food would last. All of that would take her less time than mixing up the powdered eggs into breakfast, leaving her more than enough time to obsess over the decision to repeat last night's sleeping bag aerobics.

The big question: Could she spend time in his sleeping bag without letting her heart get involved? Possibly, since half of the time she wanted to take a very large stick and beat the pompous out of him. Of course, then he'd smile or roll an *r* and she'd get hot all over, like I-want-you-right-now hot. She'd never been a love-'em-and-leave-'em sort of woman. On the other hand, roughing it in the desert and acting as a wrangler was not how she usually thought of herself…anymore. After the last rightsizing—being laid off, by another name—she'd had enough in severance to take a break. She hadn't really planned to go all cowgirl again, but that was how it'd worked out, helping Jessie and Olympia with their stock. It had all felt so familiar, but had it been right?

She'd promised herself she would have a different life than her parents and siblings. She wanted to make a living that didn't involve broken bones or shoveling manure. She'd found communications at college and never looked back. She'd been as good at that as hanging on to a bronc. Now, with so much time gone since she'd worn a suit, could she go back to the high-rises and the strict corporate hierarchy? But if not that, then what? That was the biggest, scariest question she'd ever asked herself. Jones crawled from the tent, a ray of sun glinting off his auburn hair. "Coffee?"

"Give me ten minutes. I thought you'd want tea." She sneaked a glance. Why did his shadowed jaw and slightly flattened hair look sexy? It should just look messy. He was stretching and…well…just wow. That was a lot of fine man that she'd ridden like— "I'm making eggs. If you want something else, get it from the packs." She concentrated on the camp stove and brewing coffee. Obviously, she needed the caffeine to get her brain working at full capacity and back in control of her lady parts. Or maybe they were cowgirl parts, because they certainly weren't acting ladylike.

Without warning, Jones's scent and arms surrounded her. He buried his face in her nape, and his words warmed her skin. "I want you for breakfast."

Her body softened back against him and she vibrated with excitement. "But I thought you needed coffee."

"I need you."

That should have sounded cheesy, but, no, she melted, turned and reached up to pull his mouth down onto hers.

THE PAST THREE DAYS had been a combination of hot wrestling in the sleeping bags at night and daytime drudgery of trying to find the landmarks Jones's materials had noted, along with one or two sketchy GPS coordinates. On top of that, the weather had been un-Arizona-like with rain and gray skies. Then yesterday afternoon, Reese had stepped wrong and injured his leg, and that was followed by another monsoon. There had been no question that they needed to head back to the ranch.

Her little crew had stopped just now because instead of a dry wash below them, a river filled the space. She shouldn't have been surprised, which didn't mean that she was happy about the landscape change. On the plus side, if they swung west, they should be able to cross at a spot where the arroyo widened and the water would be shallower and calmer. Where they stood now, the torrent of water squeezed into a narrow channel that looked like the black diamond of white-water rapids. With Reese limping and walking slowly, the extra mileage would take them two hours out of their way.

"What?" Jones asked, swigging from his canteen. At least they had plenty of water.

"We're going to have to make a big semicircle to a wide spot in the arroyo where it should be safe to cross."

He patted Joe's withers. "My man here can make it. Reese can swim, can't he?"

"It's not just the depth. The water here is running fast, really fast. Even Brownie couldn't swim those rapids."

She tugged on Reese's lead to get the burro moving. He walked three steps before balking and leaning back on his haunches. Great. He decided now was the time to act up. "I'm out of grain, so unless you

want to try and live off cactus, you'd better cooper-
ate." Reese eyed her, shook his head hard and finally
stepped after her. He plodded along with only a little
limp. Her horse sighed. They were tired, too. They
had been moving since early morning. On top of that,
the horses were weighed down with what had been
on Reese's back, to baby his bad leg. It was going to
be a long, miserable ride. It didn't help that she kept
feeling twinges of private muscles that had been given
a workout. Worse. Those muscles were sending zing-
ing messages that said, *Hey, another round of "hide
the salami" might make me feel better.* She'd never
imagined muscles could be such liars.

"Does this happen often?"

She was startled by Jones's voice as she argued
with her aching muscles. "What?" she asked guilt-
ily, for a second imagining that he knew what her
muscles had been suggesting.

"The rain and flooding."

"Not often this time of year, but in the summer,
flooding happens often enough. That's why there are
arroyos, washes and dry rivers. Phoenix has a whole
system of canals and parks to deal with runoff."

"The ground is like a sponge in the Highlands. It
can take in a lot of moisture, although we have small
waterfalls and streams that crop up after particularly
heavy rains."

She nodded. "You'll see. By tomorrow or the next
day, you wouldn't even know that there had been
any rain."

They plodded along for another twenty minutes
in silence—not a tense silence but not totally comfortable, either. She turned to ask him about the tar-

tan he'd worn on their first meeting and noticed that
Reese had drifted closer than she liked to the lip of
the arroyo. Sure-footed or not, the edges of arroyos
could be undercut by the water and collapse without warning.

"Eee-awh," Reese protested as she pulled on his
lead rope.

"Stupid donkey," Lavonda said, giving another tug.

Before she could tell him no, Jones got down off
his horse, walked up behind the animal and gave a
push on his hindquarters. For a moment, Reese stood
frozen. Lavonda could see a disaster rushing toward
them. "Jones, step away. Reese doesn't like to have
his—" That's all she got out before hell broke loose.
The burro kicked out his back legs, catching Jones
in the thighs. His horse skittered away and cantered
off. The giant Scot yelled and dropped to the ground
nearly over the edge of the arroyo. Lavonda jumped
from Brownie, dropping Reese's lead to get to Jones,
who was close enough to roll into the water as he
clutched his legs, swearing and in obvious pain. Reese
let out a series of ear-piercing brays, which were followed by unsettled whinnies from Brownie. Lavonda
looked over her shoulder to tell Reese to shut it just
as the edge of the arroyo disintegrated and the burro
disappeared. "Reese!" she screamed, and lunged to
capture the lead. It was gone.

She raced to the edge. The burro clung to the side
of the arroyo about five feet from where he'd fallen.
The whites of his eyes showed in terror as he brayed
frantically. Lavonda lay down on the ground, reaching out to catch his halter, but he thrashed away. She

feared his frantic movements would dislodge his unstable perch.

"Out of the way," Jones said with authority.

"Get a rope," she snapped. "I can lasso him."

Jones bumped her out of the way. With the large span of his arms, he easily reached the burro's head, catching the halter and dragging Reese toward him. The burro instinctively kicked out his legs to find purchase. Instead, they smashed away the small shelf of dirt on the side of the arroyo. Jones's muscles bunched as he took most of the donkey's weight on his shoulder. "Get the rope," he said through gritted teeth. She froze for a moment. "Now." Then she was off, because both Reese and Jones were in trouble. If the donkey kept thrashing, he'd either damage Jones's shoulder or pull the man into the arroyo. She chased down Brownie, who'd trotted fifty feet away. She dug through her packs and unearthed a coil of rope with knotted ends. Reese gave another loud bray and Brownie took off. Damn it.

"Hush, now," Jones crooned to the donkey. "Wee man, you need to stop your thrashing. Hush."

Lavonda took a deep breath, allowing his calm voice to stop the shaking in her hands. The knots gave. As she ran, she made a quick loop. Fortunately, she'd had to use a regular saddle on Reese to pack up their equipment. If she could catch the horn, she could use her body weight to hold Reese until Jones could get into a better position. Between the two of them and with a little help from Reese, they should be able to pull him up the slope. Then she heard it, even over the rush of the water. A bray, a large splash, nearly drowning out the yell and another splash. They were both gone. She raced to the edge. Maybe the water wasn't as deep as she thought or running as fast. She scanned the desert for the horses. Crappedy crap. It was her and her muscle power that would save Jones and Reese.

She scanned down the slope, then moved her gaze downstream. Jones held Reese's halter so the burro's head and white-rimmed eyes were just above the water. Jones went under and popped back up. Lavonda ran.

Chapter Seven

Damn it, man. Let the animal go. Save yourself. Jones couldn't be that rational with the thrashing, braying donkey fighting for its life. At the same time, instinct kicked in. He tried to touch bottom while keeping his head out of the fast-moving water.

"Jones," Lavonda yelled from somewhere above him. "Catch the rope." His mouth filled with water when he swirled into an eddy that pushed the dirty, grit-filled water up and over his head. He kicked out his legs and his head popped up just as a wave of water broke over him. He coughed and gagged. The donkey no longer thrashed. He glanced at the little animal, who looked calmer, eyes intent. He glanced at the bank. Lavonda stood with a rope raised over her head, whirling it in a circle.

"Catch," she yelled as she released the circle. He watched its lazy path toward him and reached out. The loop landed a foot away. As the noise of the water suddenly increased, he turned his gaze forward. The arroyo narrowed further and debris had accumulated. They sped up as the water's power increased. Even if he'd been able to plant his feet, Jones didn't think he could have stood against the pull. The burro had his head aimed at dry land. Jones followed along, kicking his legs and moving his arm to help steer them toward the bank. The water looked less turbulent there. Lavonda yelled again. "Hold on to Reese. I'm going to rope him." The loop flew again. This time it landed and tightened on the horn of the saddle. He watched as the tiny woman leaned her body back against his weight and the burro's. He kept working at stopping their downstream momentum. The white water sucked him and the struggling donkey forward and into the debris. Jones's head went under again, then his hand lost its death grip on the burro's halter. He heard the faint sound of Lavonda's voice.

Minutes, eternities later Jones felt firm earth under him and he could breathe. Alive? Dead?

"Jones." Alive. That was Lavonda's voice, frantic, high and piercing. Reese held the fabric of his sleeve in his teeth and tugged. Then, he let that go to put Jones's wrist in his mouth. What the— "Jones, don't move. I'm coming down to you."

Reese tugged again. Jones's arm dropped to the ground. He felt dizzy but had enough energy to crawl out of the water. He let his head hang down, drawing in gulps of air. Bruises he'd gotten in the tumble through the water throbbed.

"Damn it, Jones. There's no way down. Can you two walk along the edge? The arroyo looks like it widens a few hundred feet down. I should be able to help you out there."

He squinted up into the sun that radiated around Lavonda's head. "Hey," he said. "You've got a halo." He laughed and hacked up dirty water, spitting grit from his mouth.

"Did you hit your head? Jones, look at me."

He smiled up at her because, damn it, he'd survived. "Ee-awh," Reese brayed at both of them.

"Jones, use Reese to stand. You won't need to walk far."

"I'll crush him."

"You won't. Reese carries packs heavier than you."

All of Jones's muscles quivered and his left arm didn't work. Good thing he was right-handed, he thought dreamily, using that arm to lever himself up as he ignored Reese's donkey breath on the back of his neck, until donkey teeth grabbed his collar. The little animal must think it was a mother cat and him the kitten. Jones chuckled.

"Stand up, sweetie," Lavonda said, lying on the ground and looking down at him, her cartoon-princess eyes wide and worried. Why worried? He was fine now. He'd even stood up. He and his mate Reese were going to walk out of this.

Jones swayed a moment on his jelly-filled legs before instinctively putting his hand out to steady himself against the little donkey. Reese grunted, then took a step forward.

"That's it, Jones. Hold on to Reese. Remember, he's a trail burro. He knows what he's doing."

"He's a pixie's steed."

"What?" Lavonda asked, that worried tone returning.

"You're a pixie and this is your noble steed." Jones patted Reese and laughed. The sun beat down on his head. Damn. He'd lost his lucky hat. He'd liked that hat.

"Jones, you're not making any sense. Just keep walking, honey. Not far and I can help you."

"With your pixie dust?"

"Let Reese guide you. That's it. Not far now."

Jones wondered why she sounded farther away. Had she decided to fly above them? He looked up and nearly lost his grip on Reese.

"Jones," Lavonda snapped. "You hold on to that burro and walk. Now."

He automatically snapped his attention to her. Not flying. She stood above him. "You're closer. Did you get bigger? Or did I get smaller? Is this *Alice in Wonderland*?"

"Follow Reese. You're almost there."

He looked at the burro. The animal turned its head to him and winked. Really. He'd winked. He must be a pixie steed. He didn't remember any of the books he'd ever seen showing a donkey as pixie transport, but then none of the pixies he'd ever seen had breasts like Lavonda's. Maybe American pixies were different.

"Jones, stop with the pixies. Come on. Three more steps and you can sit down."

Now, Lavonda stood on one side under his arm and he had his other braced on Reese. "I'm good. No need."

"Don't let go." Her voice snapped across his brain.

He tried to straighten, but that made things go out of focus so he shuffled along. Finally, blessedly, he wasn't moving and was horizontal. He took a deep breath, sighed and drifted into a nice cushy place that held the hint of pixie dust.

WELL, SHIT AND HELLFIRE. Jones was safely out of the arroyo. Yeah. He lay stretched out on the ground, not moving. Big and immovable. How was she supposed to get him back to civilization? He might not be unconscious, just asleep from exhaustion. She looked at his pale face, noticing again the naughty-boy sprinkling of freckles across his nose and cheeks. Had he hit his head? Done some other damage? She had no idea. Basic first aid she could do. She pushed Reese's questing nose away. The donkey nibbled at the ends of Jones's damp hair.

Lavonda grasped the man's shoulder and shook him. He smiled but didn't open his eyes. How far were they from the ranch? Miles. She scanned the horizon for the horses and saw them in the far distance. No way could she get his deadweight onto either of those animals. Could she leave the two of them here and walk out for help? Probably. She could rig up shelter from the sun. She watched Jones's lips move. They abruptly pulled into a fierce frown, his brows slamming down toward his closed eyes. That had to be a good sign, right? His face couldn't be doing that if he was in a coma.

First things first, check the phone. If she could make a call and give coordinates, then it was probably best to stick around. One decision down. She unearthed her phone. Thank God for solar-powered chargers. She had juice and a faint signal. Not a reliable connection but hopefully enough to make a call. Nine-one-one or Olympia? Nothing seemed broken, and Olympia could make it faster than the emergency crews, plus she could bring a trailer for the horses and Reese.

"Hey, Olympia." Lavonda tried to sound casual.

"What's up? This is a bad connection."

"I know. I'm out—"

"Aren't you on the trail?" Olympia said at the same time.

"Let me talk. There's been an accident."

"Are you okay?"

"Just listen. Jones, the professor I was guiding, fell in an arroyo trying to rescue Reese. I think he may have hit his head. Anyway, I can't get him to mount up. We need a ride. I can give you coordinates. Can you—"

"Of course. I'll have to bring the kid, but give me the numbers."

Lavonda read out the coordinates twice and then hung up and cried, just a little, because cowgirls didn't cry even if they broke an arm or a heart. They did not cry. First rule of rodeo.

She sucked in a long deep breath, then turned to Reese and Jones. The donkey dozed and Jones hadn't moved. He'd lost his hat. She needed to get him into the shade. She trudged across the open ground toward the grazing horses. They had the supplies, including the tent canvas she needed to rig up an awning. They had at least two hours, maybe more, before her friend showed up.

LAVONDA CHECKED THE phone again for bars and the time. They'd passed the two-hour mark. She should have called 911. Jones hadn't moved and his face had smoothed into a nonexpression. She dialed Olympia's number and the phone showed failed call. No signal. Where had the bars gone, damn it? She reminded herself calmly that signals were fickle this far from a tower. "Everything is fine," she said out loud. "Jones has shade. The animals have water."

Drink. She'd gotten the donkey water but hadn't had any herself and neither had Jones. Pulling out the insulated canteen, she took a sip, followed by long swallows. She hadn't realized she was so thirsty. Stupid, she told herself. She'd been harping on Jones about staying hydrated.

"Jones," she said, giving his shoulder a little push. He didn't respond. She tried again, and this time his lids fluttered. "Jones, come on. Take a drink."

"Jings."

Crap. He was delirious, not making sense. "Jones," she said, sharply this time. "Wake up."

"I'm up," he mumbled, and took her hand. She laughed in relief. Jones frowned and glared from slitted eyes that reminded her of Cat. She laughed harder, until tears rolled down her cheeks.

"ONE, TWO, THREE." Jones counted out each lift of the grain bag over his head. Sweat gathered at his temples. He needed to build up the muscles in the shoulder that the donkey had nearly pulled from its joint. "Twenty," he gasped moments later, dropped the bag onto the stack in the corner and turned to Lavonda, who stood looking at him. "Did you need something?"

"Just dropping off Cat. She was being annoying. Did you take your allergy meds?" She cocked her head and asked, "What the hell are you doing?"

"I would think that was obvious."

"If I'd known that you wanted to heft stuff around, I would have gotten you to clean out the stalls, and then you could have cleared the brush from the second corral. Maizey is supposed to do that, but the university is using her to clear the outdoor labs."

"Maizey?"

"The goat. They're good for keeping invasive plants and brush in check. It was an experiment started by the previous owners."

Jones looked her up and down, knowing his face was hidden by the shadows. Good thing, because he had something in mind. "The sacks are fine, but not heavy enough."

"Absolutely not." She shook her head and started to back away.

He tried to look innocent as he stepped toward her. "I signed up for another game. I need to stay in condition."

"I thought you were focused on your work."

"Training for the games gives me a focus so my brain can wander down new paths. While lifting weights or running, I often come up with new connections. It has been posited that allowing the brain to—"

"I am not your barbell. If you need extra weights, find a gym."

She turned and he made his move, grabbing her and lifting her in one clean motion into a bench press. He watched carefully to make sure he didn't bash her head into the barn beams. That would be bad form. "One," he said as he allowed her to drop down and then pushed her upward. "Two."

"Jones, put me down."

"Three," he said as she moved again. She grabbed

at his wrist. "I won't drop you. I've lifted much heavier weights, though you're more solid than I would have thought." She pinched the skin on his wrist hard. "Ouch. Four." He blew out a breath before pushing her back toward the roof. "You do realize that if I drop you, it will hurt."

"I rode broncs. I'm not afraid of a little hurt."

"Ha. Five."

"I mean it. Put me down."

"Two sets of ten. Six."

"No."

"Seven."

"Cat. Reese. Get him," she yelled, wiggling and stopping when his grip wobbled. "You won't think this is funny when I get back at you. No more fancy beer. No more Hobnobs." Cat yowled at the last. Until he stored the treats in the freezer, the feline wouldn't be stopped from breaking into the kitchen cupboards and eating his supply.

"I believe…nine…that would be cruel and unusual punishment…ten. Done." He lowered her to the ground, placing her on her feet. She swayed a second. He watched carefully to make sure she didn't fall.

"You think that was funny? I know where the castration shears are."

He laughed. "That would be cutting off my…well, you know what to spite your…parts?"

"You're a pig. Men are pigs. I knew it. I've known it my whole life. You think this is funny?"

He shrugged his shoulder and stopped almost immediately. The lifting might not have been the best idea he'd had recently, not that many of his ideas in the past six months had been stellar.

He watched her expression go from annoyed to mad. "Did the doctor say that you were allowed to lift weights?" He tried the shrug again. "I thought you were smart."

"I am. My shoulder is fine. I need to strengthen the muscles to keep the joint stable. I separated it years ago, so it's prone to injury. It's nice to know you care, though."

She snorted and pushed Cat away with her foot. "I saved your bacon, didn't I? I didn't do that so you'd end up in the hospital."

He stepped close enough to catch her scent of chili and spring leaves. "Have I thanked you for that?" He massaged her shoulders. He had thanked her more than once in the bed they'd been sharing.

"You will thank me by not reinjuring yourself, because you're expected to find those beans."

"I'll find the damned beans." That broke the mood. He'd been doing well enough ignoring that he hadn't made progress on finding Kincaid's Cache while getting deeper into his lie. "You don't trust me to be careful?"

She shook her head. "You're a man, so, no, I don't trust you."

"Condemning all men?"

"I've known a lot of men."

"Really?" He knew what she meant. That did not stop a spurt of heated anger from lodging just under his breastbone.

"I have a brother and father, and have worked at corporations and competed in rodeos. I have first-hand knowledge of how often men don't know when to call it quits."

He made a noise that she could interpret however she wanted.

"You only have a short time in Arizona and you want to make sure you can take advantage of every day. I know you've lost time in the field, resting your shoulder, which bench-pressing bags of feed—"

"And petite ladies."

"I'm petite now?"

"I may have more experience with determining the age of wheat grains, but even I know not to comment on that."

"How is the search for a new guide going?" She obviously wanted to change the subject.

"I have been considering the efficacy of hiring a new guide," he said in his best professor tones. Another lie. He hadn't called any of the names that Stanley had given him. "You and I worked well in the field. You have the experience and—"

"If you think that would be best *and* aren't making the decision because we shared a tent."

"Just a tent?" He stepped to her.

"Sorry. An air mattress."

"You sound upset."

"I just want to be clear about what we're talking about."

"What are we talking about?" He suddenly wasn't so clear.

"Crap," she said with feeling. "You're going to make me say it. We're talking about being lovers."

"I thought that was already established."

"Could you sound less like a professor and more like a man?"

"Do you want me to growl or roll my *r*'s?" he asked, doing both. She shivered. He'd found out both of those made her hot.

"Boundaries. We need boundaries," she breathed.

"What boundaries?"

"In the field, I'm the guide. We'll keep our relationship private, because I don't want Daddy or Danny here with shotguns."

"Do people really do that?" He might actually be in the Wild West, after all. More of his childhood dreams coming true.

"Close enough." She firmed her chin.

"As long as you promise to keep your ideas about training to yourself."

"I promise to supply you with Hobnobs and teach you how to clean out the stalls."

"I would think a visitor would be given a pass on barn work."

"Houseguests would offer to lend a hand."

"That puts us at an impasse. I'll wrestle you for it."

"Really. You think that's fair. Look at you. Look at me."

"Thumb wrestle?"

"Tickle torture."

"No. No tickling."

"What? You're a big Highlander with tough-as-nails muscles. What's wrong with a little tickling?" She reached out and tested the ticklishness of his armpit. He tried to push her away, but he couldn't stop laughing. She kept at it until he could barely catch his breath and collapsed with her on top of him. "Kissing is allowed, right?" she whispered against his lips.

"Most definitely yes." His arms came up and around her to hold her tightly against him. This right here was enough for now.

Chapter Eight

Lavonda sipped her coffee and looked out from the back patio, enjoying the view of the mountains, the muted browns and greens of the desert. She could see herself staying here, settling in. At Hacienda Bunuelos, she'd found her first "home" since she'd become an adult. Not that she'd nested, not like Jessie and Olympia. The ranch with its out-of-place veranda and the softly rounded edges of the old-fashioned adobe was the kind of property that she could make into so much. Transforming the house and upgrading the stables, though, would cost money. Money she didn't have after living off her savings since she'd been downsized. She could get the money she needed if she went back to work in corporate communications—not exactly her calling, but she was darned good at it.

She'd done a little discreet digging and the university might be willing to sell the property. Of course, to buy it, she needed a job, thus another reason to put out her résumé as soon as her commitment to Jones… to the university and Gwen ended. It would be over by fall, and by then Lavonda would have a business plan, like the dozens she'd created for her various employers. Maybe the property could be her retirement career, something appropriate like a retreat-style bed-and-breakfast or dude ranch. Both had possibilities and neither would include Jones. Anyway, he wasn't her type. She went for suits and neatly trimmed hair.

Right now, she needed to call Olympia. Lavonda couldn't keep ignoring her friend's voice mails and texts. She would have to stick with her story that Gwen had forced her to stay on as trail boss to the jolly green Scot.

More importantly, she had a "job" for Olympia, who could use the cash. While Jones and Lavonda went out into the desert again, someone needed to check on the ranch and its inhabitants—Cat and Maizey. The university had agreed to pay Olympia the going rate. Plus, Cat had not liked the man who'd come to take care of the ranch the last time. The other part of her responsibility would be checking on the petroglyphs and one other site.

"How's it going?" Lavonda said when Olympia answered the phone.

"Why did I help talk Spence into adopting this puppy?"

"Because you didn't want to disappoint your stepson or your sister?"

Her friend laughed. "You got that right. My sister, however, did not explain to me when she talked us into adopting the puppy that he would grow up to be a small-sized pony. What's up?"

"I've got to take the Scotsman back out into the desert. They still haven't found another guide."

"And they won't, since you're free."

"I get to live at this great ranch."

"Uh-huh."

"I've done such a good job of keeping Jones alive that I'll probably get all kinds of recommendations. Maybe I should become a full-time guide."

"If that makes you happy."

"It might," Lavonda said, and felt herself relax just a little. Talking with Olympia was like talking with her sister, Jessie, without the big-sister I-know-what's-best-for-you attitude.

"So, how long? Cal liked Cat when he visited and is trying to convince Spence we need a kitten who will grow into a cat, to keep our barn safe from mice. Spence said no, of course. We've already got the dog."

"The only thing that Cat has caught so far has been a scorpion and Hobnobs."

"Hobnobs? What kind of animal is that?"

"It's a cookie. Scottish."

"Scottish, huh? How is your Highlander?"

"He's not mine and he's fine."

"Fine as in *fine* or as in *fiiine*?"

"None of your business."

"Then he's *fiiine*. Give me all of the details."

"No details. I'm just his trail guide."

"Uh-uh. I don't believe that—"

"And he'll be leaving by the fall."

"Then what?"

"I have plans."

"Like going to Scotland."

"Not going to Scotland."

"It looks beautiful."

"Arizona is home."

"Is it? You haven't settled anywhere."

"I'm living at Hacienda Bunuelos."

"Temporarily. If you wanted to follow the professor to Scotland you could…you should."

Lavonda didn't want to even think about the appeal of that suggestion. "First, whatever may or may not be going on between Jones and me will *not* end with a walk down the aisle. Second, I really like living on the ranch, and the university might—"

"Might what?"

"Might be willing to sell."

"That would be great, Lavonda. It would be nice to have you so close, and I know Jessie would love it if you finally settled down nearby. Your mama and daddy, too."

"It's not like I'd live here right away. More like a retirement place. Or second career. Don't say anything. I haven't spoken with Gwen, and I'm still working on the logistics."

"What would you do? Raise broncs?"

"Still working that out."

"Lavonda, honey," Olympia said. "Buying the ranch isn't going to fill up that hole Jones will leave when he goes back to Scotland. You know that, right?"

"This isn't about Jones. Everyone is after me about my future. Well, I've come up with a plan for my future. It's buying this ranch." There. She'd said it. Olympia and her whole family could go pound sand. She was buying the ranch and then she'd…well, she'd figure that out.

"I told you, I'd love to have you so close by, but not if you're not happy. I can tell that Jones is more than a colleague, no matter what you've said. That's why

I know the ranch won't fill the space that he leaves in your life."

"He's not. We're not. I'll call you with exact dates as soon as I have them. Bye." Lavonda hung up before her friend could say more. A crackle of plastic caught her attention. Cat sat across the kitchen with an empty packet of Hobnobs. Jones must have forgotten to put them in the freezer. Lavonda wanted to scold the animal but couldn't because tears clogged her throat. What would she and Cat do when Jones was gone? And he would be going. They had another trip planned, although they'd been putting it off until his shoulder completely healed and maybe because the bed was much more comfortable than the hard ground. He'd been going out on his own to various well-catalogued and -explored sites as part of his research. He'd also driven to other extensively documented locations, staying over as he needed to. She certainly didn't wait for him to come home when he had classes to teach or was happy that he'd cut at least two of those trips short to get home early.

She wasn't interested in a forever kind of relationship. Since her last downsizing, she hadn't been able to commit to a career, so how could she commit to a person? Plus, even *if* she wanted something more permanent, Jones lived in Scotland. Buying the ranch meant she would call Arizona home.

Or maybe Jones would stay and get a permanent job. He'd talked about how much he loved the West and he'd fit right in. Sure his life had been in Scotland, but who was to say that was the place that best suited him?

Jones sneezed, cursed and rolled from bed in one motion. Lavonda didn't stir. He pushed Cat out of the bedroom with one foot as he picked up his buzzing phone on the way to the kitchen, where he could take another allergy pill.

"Yes," he said as he flipped on lights.

"You took the journal, Ross," Iain accused.

Why hadn't he checked his caller ID? And why did his real name sound so odd? "Hello to you."

"The American Kincaid's journal is missing."

Jones pulled the pill bottle from the cabinet.

His brother's annoyed voice came over the phone again. "I knew there was another reason you headed to Arizona."

Jones had sufficiently gathered his wits. Reality was not what he wanted to face in the middle of the night after waking pressed up against Lavonda and thinking that maybe they should try another round of…what did she call it?…*hide the*—

"Are you drunk?" his brother asked.

"You woke me. It's the middle of the night."

"What the hell do you think you're doing?"

"I'm investigating the use of—"

"Bollocks. You're after Kincaid's Cache and its blasted treasure."

"You saw the paperwork. I know you did. In fact, you approved the research."

"I approved your investigation of the Hohokam and their use of beans as an alternate source of protein and how that discovery affected the development of their social structure as well as how the culture may be reflective of those in northern Europe. I did not approve you going on a treasure hunt. This is not *Raiders of the Lost Ark*."

"Call me at a reasonable time of the day." Jones chugged more water with his pill. He'd been dosing himself with the allergy tablets after he and Lavonda gave up the plan to just have sex and not *sleep* together. Not that he'd ever imagined that was going to work. No one wanted to have great sex, then crawl back to their own bed. They both tried to keep Cat out of the house and especially the bedrooms, but she found her way into spaces that shouldn't accommodate her bulk.

"This is your last chance."

"Don't be dramatic."

"I'm telling you the university will sack you if you choose Hollywood over substance again."

"Hollywood?"

"It's like you've decided that those ridiculous movies are real."

"The source for the Viking material had been reliable in the past. Not every project finds success. You know that."

"Of course, I know that. But then not every dig becomes a YouTube video. How could you have been fooled?"

"I was not fooled. Obviously, whatever had been stored there had been removed. But after the video, you and the university wouldn't give me the opportunity to explore that avenue."

"The university had already... I tried... I did not call you to talk about the dolls, Ross."

"It seems that way to me."

"Let's play out a hypothetical scenario," Iain said.

Jones would give his brother another three minutes of his attention. "You've deciphered the journals and are searching the desert. You find the cave. It's filled with the treasure or Egyptian artifacts or whatever the hell he said. Then what? Wait a moment. I forgot to add to the hypothetical that the archaeologist lied to—"

"I did not lie."

"You are *not* searching for beans as you indicated to the university."

"I can't do two things at once?"

Jones wanted to throw the glass because his smug arse of a brother did that to him. Iain was the older and obviously smarter brother. He did well academically and didn't have any inclination to ride horses too fast or toss a caber. "I'm going back to bed, Iain. I don't know what delusion you're working under. I'm doing serious academic work."

"You're a bad liar, always have been, which is why you never would have made chairman. You've got to flatter. None of that nonsense about being a 'straight shooter.' I'm warning you—another treasure hunt will end your chances of *any* university taking you on. They want academics, not Indiana Jones. I'm just trying to point out the realities of the situation. I don't see how I can save you this time."

"I don't need saving because I am doing research in Arizona."

"So you say." His brother paused. "Truly. I'm only trying to help you. My God, man, you're my little brother."

"Like you did when you told the reporter after Dolly-Acropolis that I'd been diagnosed with a short-term mental illness?"

"That might not have been the best choice of words."

"I may not have all of my evidence from this one trip. I may need an extension."

"I won't cover for you, because your delusions could ruin my career."

"I have already told you that my investigations—"

"I might believe you if the journal was not missing, and if I had not seen the files on—"

"You hacked into my computer?" This had gone too far even for Iain.

"No hacking. You worked on the university server."

"I am doing my stated research."

"Saying it often enough does not make it true. I'm your brother. I know you."

He heard footfalls in the hallway and instantly lowered his voice. "I've got to go."

Lavonda's sleepy voice said from just behind him, "Who are you talking to? Is there something wrong? It's the middle of the night. Why is Cat sitting on your foot?"

Jones swore and barely heard his brother's comment. "A woman. This is about a woman."

"Iain, I'm ringing off."

"Ross, don't let a pair of—"

"Don't say anything more. Goodbye, Iain." Jones turned off the phone before his brother made a remark that would completely destroy whatever very thin thread of filial connection remained between them. He nudged Cat from his foot, and the animal strolled away, tail in the air, toward his room. Damn. Maybe they should go to Lavonda's room at the back of the ranch house in the separate quarters. Perhaps Cat had not contaminated that area too thoroughly.

Lavonda snuggled up to him. "Who was that?" she asked again, her face laid comfortably against his chest.

"No one."

She shook her head. "A long conversation for no one."

"It's late."

"Sounded like a sibling."

He stiffened.

"Something's wrong, isn't it?"

"Just the usual."

She burrowed into his arms, holding on tight. "You don't get along?" she asked quietly.

"Just the usual brother…stuff."

"Family. Can't live with them and you can't black-mail them."

"Something like that."

Lavonda pulled back enough to look into his face. Her brows arched upward. "Much worse than he borrowed your Ninja Turtle shield and nunchaku."

Jones hesitated. He wanted to explain to her how his family wasn't like hers. She might complain about her brother and sister and her parents and all of the extended family, but it was the sort of complaining based in the sure knowledge that every one of those people could be counted on to have her back. Iain and he had been competing so long that he could never count on his brother. "Iain took my job." *Shite*. Why had he blurted that out?

"What job? You have a job."

"I should be chair of the department. It was the

first time in my life that I would actually have beaten him at something. But then, he... I—"

She waited for him to say more, but he couldn't. He couldn't reveal anything more because then he'd be forced to explain exactly why he was in Arizona. "Let's go back to bed." The pit of his stomach dropped when she wouldn't look away from him.

"That's not all of it. What else?"

"What else could there be? Isn't that enough? It's an age-old story, right? Younger brother losing out to older brother, resentment, all of that."

Her wide honey-brown eyes darkened a shade. "You're lying about something."

"I told you. We're competitive. He called to—"

"That's it. I couldn't figure out why everything seemed wrong, but why would your highly intelligent brother call you in the middle of the night?"

"He's bad at maths?"

She shook her head hard enough to make her hair fly. He stepped in to kiss her, to distract her. He was tired and annoyed and he had exactly zero lies at his disposal.

"No. Tell me what he wanted."

He stopped, put his hands on his hips and went for his best Clint Eastwood squint. "I've told you it's nothing."

She crossed her arms over her chest, pulling tight the pink tank top. "I'm not moving until you tell me."

He licked his lips, opened his mouth and closed it, then rearranged his stance to cover his soaring interest in her clearly visible-through-the-fabric nipples.

"Dear Lord," she said. "You're turned-on."

"What did you expect?"

She returned his squint with a glare. "I expect you to act like an intelligent man and answer my questions."

"It's late." Late was right. Too late to turn back and tell her the full truth. Too late for him to get back his reputation with a cache that he lied to find?

"We're not done."

"I am, although I'd certainly like to have you again." He turned away.

"What kind of crap is that? You can't ignore my questions, then expect to get busy with me. Good night." She turned in the opposite direction to go to her own bedroom at the back of the house.

Fan-freakin'-tastic. His brother had not only called to taunt him about his career but also managed to mess up his very pleasant interlude with his cowgirl pixie. Great. What was next?

"Yee-owl." Cat was back on his foot, squinting up at him—maybe she'd watched a lot of Eastwood, too—then she opened her mouth again and vomited Hobnobs.

"What the—" he yelled, and instinctively kicked out, striking Cat, who screeched her displeasure before turning to attack his leg.

Chapter Nine

Lavonda heard growls and a deep-throated yell. She paused a moment, ready to turn off the bedroom light. Then she heard Jones shout out with anguish, "Bloody hell."

She sighed, knowing Cat had done something to the Scotsman. She was the ranch's caretaker and Jones's, too. Lavonda made her way back to the kitchen, where Jones glared at Cat, his fists clenched at his side. "What's the trouble? Did she eat—" Bloody gouges on his legs stopped her. What had the animal done? "I'll get the first-aid kit." She hurried to the bathroom for peroxide and bandages. Cat's scratches could be wicked.

"Sit," she told Jones, directing him to a chair.

"I need a whiskey. A large one, before you do anything."

She didn't argue. He didn't seem to be in the kind of mood where she could reason with him. Better to get him something to drink, clean the scratches, then send him to bed...alone.

"The scratches aren't that bad. At least you won't need a rabies shot. Cat's vaccinated." She stared at the cheap glass filled with Jones's expensive whiskey.

"I don't want to drink alone." He poured another glass and pushed it to her.

She reluctantly took the three fingers of whiskey, tapped her glass against his and took a sip. She was enough of a cowgirl to not cough, but, Baby Jesus and His Donkey, it was strong. She got back to playing nurse. "This shouldn't hurt. I just want to make sure they're cleaned well."

Jones sat and pulled a kitchen towel over his lap. She dabbed at the cuts. He didn't move or make a noise. She was nearly impressed because she knew how much it hurt to clean out the animal's scratches. He was pretty good at the stoic-cowboy thing, like her brother and father. Of course, he also went for the Clint Eastwood squint. She'd seen him trying it on Cat. She smiled.

"What?" he asked, his glass nearly empty of whiskey as he put it on the table.

"Nothing. Almost done."

"You're good. Barely felt a thing."

"I doubt that. I know how much the peroxide burns. But cat scratch fever is a real thing. Wouldn't want you to be too sick to finish your research, Jones."

"We wouldn't want that."

She really looked at him. Something in his face was different. What had his brother said on the call? "Everything okay at home?"

"As right as a summer monsoon."

She looked up at him, and saw his broad grin and the spark in his green eyes. She turned back to the final swipe of peroxide. "Are you sure that's your first whiskey?"

"Absolutely positive, darlin'."

"Was that supposed to be John Wayne?"

"Maybe? You've barely touched your drink."

"I've had enough. I'm more a beer girl myself."

"Not that American piffle?"

No longer a cowpoke, he sounded foreign and offended. "I go for mass-market, pretend Mexican-beer options."

"I know you drank one of my stouts."

"Guilty. Well, Jones, you're patched up and—"

"It's not 'Jones,'" he said, very serious.

"What?" His eyes looked too clear for him to be drunk.

"It's a nickname. One my family and friends gave me because I was so good at archaeology. My real name is Ross Nigel Meredith Kincaid. If you search for Ross Kincaid, you'll find me."

What was he saying? That she'd been sleeping with a man she didn't even know? "Are you on the run from the law?"

"I wish. I'm on the run from the damned internet."

Crap. Her brain shifted into PR disaster mode. When she'd been working at corporations, they had plans for such disasters.

He rose from the chair as he said, "I'll get my laptop and show you. I can tell that you're coming up with something really horrible. I didn't murder anyone."

She thought she heard him say, "Except my career."

HE'D KEPT QUIET about all of this for months—why had he felt the need to confess tonight? The whiskey. Blame it on the whiskey, isn't that what you did in such situations? Damn it. He'd seen her face. She'd been hurt and scared. Of course, she had. He'd lied to her.

The coolly logical Professor Kincaid part of his brain pointed out that he hadn't lied technically. He just hadn't revealed all. Many people knew him as Jones and anyone could understand why he'd tried to distance himself from the online memes and videos making fun of the cairn of dolls. The trip to Arizona had been his chance to salvage his career and academic reputation, and to leave behind the inevitable giggles from everyone he met.

"I'll tell you—" He didn't get further because she was already intent on the screen of her phone.

"You found me?"

"Wow," she said, not moving her gaze from her phone. "Dolly-Acropolis? Archaeologists often don't find what they're looking for. What was the big deal?"

He opened his mouth to answer.

She immediately broke in, "I see. You were looking for a treasure, like looking for Montezuma's gold here."

"Something like that. The university contacted television shows and newspapers. No one imagined so many journalists would show up. In retrospect, we should have waited until we were sure what we'd find."

"I'm a little confused. This doesn't seem to have anything to do with your current research. Aren't you the bean guy?"

He hadn't thought this through as well as he'd imagined. Lavonda had that effect on him. "I'm returning to my roots." In more ways than one, so it wasn't really a lie.

"Ah…oh, my, did you see the one where they put a bullwhip in your hand like Indiana Jones?"

"I've looked at all of them."

She put the phone down. He waited. She took a sip of whiskey, leaned her head back and stared at the ceiling. Good God. Why was she torturing him?

"I can't decide how annoyed I should be. Not annoyed. That's not right. How mad should I be that you lied about your name and your past?"

"Technically—"

"Don't even try. You lied. You knew you were lying, deceiving me and we…we've been intimate. I expect a certain amount of honesty."

He unglued his feet from the floor and moved toward her. She put up her hand. He stopped, sat down and picked up her hand before she could pull away. "Ask me whatever you want and I'll tell you the truth. The complete truth." Why was he promising what he couldn't give her? He wanted to erase the hurt from her face.

"So you're just in Arizona for the research?"

"To compare the bean culture of…"

She stared at him, her usually wide eyes narrowed. "You're running away?"

That hurt. "Not running away. Redeeming myself, I'd say." That was true, at least. "It's complicated."

"That's what people insist when they don't want to explain something."

"In this case, it's true. I am here to work on my research, but the complication is that my brother is chair of the department. He and I don't always see eye to

eye." Again, totally true. He and Iain hadn't agreed
on the color of sky since they were teens. It had gotten even worse as Jones had insisted he wanted to
study the American West.

"I would guess that the discovery of the dolls instead of the gold messed him up, too."

"Not that much. He ended up chairman of the department and I ended up... You saw."

"Hmm," she said, looking again at her phone. "I
should be kicking you to the curb for the way you've
treated me, but... I'm a big fan of underdogs." She
smiled sweetly, leaned forward and kissed him.
"Don't think you're totally forgiven, but I understand."

She understood now, but what would she think if
she found out the other bigger lie? Why did it matter
what she thought? Because it did. Because she was
right. She did deserve his honesty.

"I assume Gwen and Stanley know who you really are?"

"Yes, but...shite... I don't know—"

"There's more? You lied about something else?"
She pulled away and the disappointment in her eyes
nearly made him change his mind.

"More a case of not revealing all."

"I call BS."

He stood and paced three steps. The whiskey
sloshed in his stomach and his chest tightened. He
had faced a wall of cameras with a pile of dolls. He
could do this. He had to do this.

"It's about the *real* reason I came here."

"Real? You're not hunting beans?"

He rubbed his hand over his face, hoping for clarity and inspiration. He got none. "I am following the trail of a Kincaid relative who found a cache."

"He studied beans, too?" Her voice continued to be quizzical.

"No. He and a couple of other archaeologists—adventurers really—found a cave."

"What else? You said a cache. Like a treasure? Like the Lost Dutchman's Mine."

"Not exactly."

"Then what?"

"The American Kincaid—that's what we call him—sent a set of journals back to my great-great-grandfather in Scotland. They were placed in the library…but that doesn't matter. I found them and realized that the material was in code and that what the American Kincaid had found was a cache of relics stolen from a Spanish wagon train bringing treasure to the missions."

"You're looking for a hidden treasure? You've got to be kidding me."

"The journals were very clear once I broke the code."

"Did you use a secret decoder ring?"

"Beans are not going to restore my reputation or get me the chairmanship."

"I don't know a lot about academics, but I don't think following a secret treasure map is going to get you accolades."

"If what the journal revealed is true, this could be bigger than King Tut."

"Gwen and Stanley know what you're doing?"

"No," he said slowly. "I didn't want another Dolly-Acropolis. Press and everyone else watching and—"

"You have to tell them. And if you won't, I will."

YOUR PARTICIPATION IS REQUESTED!

Dear Reader,

Since you are a lover of our books – we would like to get to know you!

Inside you will find a short Reader's Survey. Sharing your answers with us will help our editorial staff understand who you are and what activities you enjoy.

To thank you for your participation, we would like to send you 2 books and 2 gifts – **ABSOLUTELY FREE!**

Enjoy your gifts with our appreciation,

Pam Powers

SEE INSIDE FOR READER'S SURVEY

For Your Reading Pleasure...

We'll send you 2 books and 2 gifts
ABSOLUTELY FREE
just for completing our Reader's Survey!

YOUR READER'S SURVEY
"THANK YOU" FREE GIFTS INCLUDE:
- ▶ 2 FREE books
- ▶ 2 lovely surprise gifts

BUSINESS REPLY MAIL
FIRST-CLASS MAIL   PERMIT NO. 717   BUFFALO, NY

POSTAGE WILL BE PAID BY ADDRESSEE

READER SERVICE
PO BOX 1867
BUFFALO NY 14240-9952

NO POSTAGE
NECESSARY
IF MAILED
IN THE
UNITED STATES

"I don't need you to do that. I'll tell Gwen and Stanley. You're right that I should be truthful." He picked up his glass to refill it with whiskey. "I'll find a new guide," Jones said. He took another sip and turned to Lavonda, wiping his face clear of expression. "I'll also stay in my own room…alone…from here on out."

"Is that so?" she asked. "Are you implying that I'm so enamored of you and your Scotsman that I can't say no on my own?"

Shite. Why couldn't she appreciate that he was protecting her? He knew she wasn't the kind of woman who slept with a man lightly.

"Stop it right now," Lavonda said, standing inches away and glaring up at him. "I can read it on your face. You think I'm naive." She poked him in the chest. "Let me tell you, Dr. Kincaid, I've traveled around the world, worked for Fortune 500 companies, and I wasn't a virgin. I understand how the world works and I don't need some *Scotsman* who imagines that he's a cowboy to protect me from myself. I'm a grown woman. So yes, you will be sleeping by yourself and if you say another word, I may just send Cat in there to keep you company."

She walked off to her bedroom, not dramatically and not hurriedly. She walked just like the adult woman she'd just told him she was. The adult, intelligent woman she was.

"Hell," he said to the kitchen. He'd imagined the stash of moldy baby dolls was bad. Child's play… He barked out a laugh, slammed back the rest of the whiskey then stood looking around the room. He wanted to…needed to… "Double hell." If he were a real cowboy, he'd go out to the barn, saddle up a horse and ride off this anger. Isn't that what the cowboys in his favorite movies did? Instead, he stood in the kitchen of a cowgirl's ranch house still arguing with himself about sleeping with his pixie.

SITTING IN GWEN'S OFFICE, Jones shifted in his seat. He'd apologized, explained himself and accepted his punishment. Why weren't they done with him?

Stanley's face remained in its stern lines. "While you will be expected to finish your contract, we will not provide any additional funding for a guide, nor will we require anyone affiliated with the university to offer his or her expertise."

"To clarify," Jones said, to prove he could out-professor the lot of them, "any forays into the desert are without a guide, unless I pay for that out of my own pocket. I am, however, still afforded the use of the ranch and its equipment?" Stanley nodded.

The campus president took up the argument, "We will also be contacting your home university about the deception—"

"There was no deception," Jones said. He and Iain might not get along but he wasn't hanging out his brother for discipline. "I am and have been following the bean research as outlined in my proposal."

Dr. Hernandez said, "We have made our decision. We will fulfill our portion of the contract and provide you housing at the ranch. We will also publicize your findings, but only after they have been thoroughly vetted by our department. Lavonda will no longer be required to be your guide as part of her obligation to the university, by the way."

Lavonda finally entered the conversation. "I would also suggest having a press release and statement available in case Dr. Kincaid's past comes up from another avenue. The students may have or will ferret this out. They are researchers, after all."

"You're right," Gwen said. "Please prepare that and bill me directly."

Lavonda nodded and turned for a moment to look at Jones. He tried to interpret her expression, but he'd lost that ability when she had found out about the lies.

"We're done here," Gwen said and stood, clearly telling everyone it was time to head out.

LAVONDA'S MINI COOPER hadn't gotten any bigger. In fact, Jones was sure it had shrunk. He sat as close to the door as he was able so he didn't accidentally brush against Lavonda. She had been silent since the meeting. He still had eight weeks remaining in the agreement. How many of those could he spend in the field? Being around Lavonda would not work out, but he needed her help to get to the cache. Since he'd been sleeping alone, he'd had plenty of time to work with the journals and was certain he'd discovered the proper landmarks about thirty miles from the ranch. A lengthy but not unreasonable horseback ride. He could take the animals by himself, but Lavonda understood how to find water and seemed to instinctively know the best paths. He couldn't ask her to help, though. Or could he?

"I know you are no longer obligated to help me," Jones said into the tense silence of the Mini about fifteen minutes from the ranch, "however, I do have more research to complete, which could be finished faster with the help of an experienced guide." He kept his voice very matter-of-fact as he went on. "The sooner I complete the research, the sooner I'll be off the ranch."

She turned her head slowly toward him. Her dark Disney-princess eyes were blank. "That would be grand."

Grand? "I've apologized. You've got to understand the situation was—"

"I understand that you're a liar. I understand that you only care about yourself. I understand that I'm going to have to lead you out into the desert again because I refuse to have your death on my head, and I want you gone as soon as possible."

"Then we're in agreement."

"In agreement, that you're a…a…jerk? Then yes."

"You have to see it from my viewpoint."

"No. I don't." She sliced through the air with her hand, swatting away his words, her eyes once again on the road. "Gwen and Stanley were clear about their expectations. Here are mine: I will be your guide. I will care for the animals and ensure that we have enough supplies. That is all."

"All right."

"I will hold you to completing your research by your deadline. Finally, I expect that you will keep anything that was not professional about our previous relationship to yourself?"

"Of course. In any case, that had nothing to do with this."

"God. You really are a cowboy. Only a cowboy could be so bullheadedly stubborn in not understanding that lying about his past and his *name* is the same as saying that I was just any old warm body in the night." She looked away from the windshield to stare at him.

Oh, God, the hurt in her wide-eyed glance tightened his stomach in self-loathing. It was for the best that all of this had come out and that she was ending things. He wanted to make sure that there was no going back. "What are those rodeo women called? Buckle bunnies?"

Her knuckles whitened on the steering wheel. "Don't say another word."

Good. He'd really made her mad now. She wouldn't imagine that they could have any sort of personal relationship. She would thank him for that when she figured out that he hadn't given up on finding the cache, no matter what she or the university thought.

Chapter Ten

"Tell me you can't come and take care of Cat," Lavonda said to Olympia as soon as the other woman answered the phone.

"Okay. I can't take care of Cat. Why am I saying this?" A faint "yes we can" in a young male voice came through the phone.

Lavonda paced in her room, ignoring Cat's glare. "Is that Cal?"

"You know how he feels about that animal. Really, why am I not able to take care of her?"

"I'm supposed to take Dr. Kincaid out on the trail. If I can't find someone to care for the animals, I won't be able to do that." It wasn't the best of excuses, but Lavonda would take anything to stay at the ranch while Jones went out into the desert and he wandered there like Moses, for all she cared. She should never have agreed to guide him in the first place. It might have been her hormones talking and she had put those in their place now.

"Dr. Kincaid…" Olympia paused. "Tell me what's going on."

"I told you the eminent archaeologist residing at

Hacienda Bunuelos will be out in the desert and needs a guide. Me."

"That's the same kilted guy that you—"

"He's the professor being hosted by the university that owns the ranch."

"Stop, Lavonda. Tell me what's going on or I'm packing everyone up—including the puppy—and coming for a visit."

"Cat heard that," Lavonda said, stalling. She looked at the feline, who really did have extra menace in her stare.

"If that threat doesn't work, I'm pulling out the big guns. I'll tell Jessie or…your mother."

Lavonda cracked. She should be better than this. A professional businesswoman should have more backbone than to cave at the thought of someone calling her mother. She told Olympia about the meeting in Gwen's office, about Jones's—or should she say Ross's—lies, and the most telling fact: Dolly-Acropolis.

"I can see why he might not want to broadcast he'd found dolls instead of gold," Olympia finally said.

"He lied."

"So?"

Lavonda could almost hear the shrug through the phone. "Let me say it again. He. Lied."

"Sounds more like he didn't reveal everything. And you're telling me that you've been completely open and honest with him about everything? Because this certainly is not about him deceiving the university. This is about him and you."

"There wasn't a him and me. We just…" Lavonda trailed off because honestly—as if anything about the situation invoked honesty—she didn't know what they *had* been.

"Of course, there was a you and him. You don't get involved—and I would say something else here, but little pitchers, big ears—if you don't feel something or want a more permanent relationship."

All of that made Lavonda want to cry, wail and beat her breasts. She didn't even care how overly dramatic that sounded. "Be that as it may," she responded, "he lied, and I want my interactions with him to be limited. Going out on the trail is not limiting my exposure to more of his lies."

"Let me try this. When you worked in PR, you never lied, right?" Olympia didn't wait for an answer. "Instead, you put the best face on things so the business could do its business. That's all Jones has done. He revamped his name and picked a glamorous new quest to move on after a disaster. It's not like he's an ax murderer. Cut him a break."

"You're my friend. You're supposed to agree with me."

"I do agree with you when you aren't being…unreasonable." Olympia sighed deeply. "You are right that he shouldn't have deceived you after you two… became close. But this is something you should understand, isn't it? Did you tell your bosses that you were bronc rider? That you'd won a buckle?"

"It never came up." Lavonda could see where this argument was leading.

"I bet even your corporate boyfriends didn't know about that. How is that any different? He just didn't reveal everything right now. Both of you were working on trusting the other."

"All right. You made your point. I'm an unreasonable, emotionally blackmailing female."

"You are making this tougher than it should be. I'm just saying that you need to put this in context, in perspective. After you do that, call me back and ask about Cat again." Olympia hung up.

Lavonda stared down at the animal in question. "Is Olympia right? Am I being overly dramatic?" Cat's eyelids closed halfway. "You're bored with this conversation, huh?"

Lavonda walked to the kitchenette and pulled out a pitcher of iced tea. She remembered Jones—not even his real name—and her... She stopped the rest of the mental rant. He'd explained that the nickname had been given to him by his brother at school. On the rodeo circuit, people gave themselves new names all the time. It wasn't about deceiving but about marking a change in their lives. She couldn't blame Jones for wanting to distance himself from his past. She'd done the same when she'd gotten rid of all of her jeans and boots, only wearing tailored suits. Didn't everyone deserve a second chance? Isn't that what the whole West had been built on? That might be a little farfetched, but she'd guess that at least a few of her ancestors had come out here to give themselves that second chance, leaving behind a life that no longer worked or that they had messed up or one of a thousand other reasons.

She called Olympia back and asked her to watch Cat and the ranch.

"I'm not going to say you were right," Lavonda said, "except you made me rethink the situation. I can give him a second chance because in the big scheme, it's not like he did anything thousands of others have not done before. I remember a girl at the rodeo who insisted that her name was Star. Her real name was Caroline. She said that was to honor Belle Starr and to let everyone know that she'd be in the money. It was also because she'd gotten into some trouble, as we found out. She was just leaving that behind, marking that she had begun a new chapter, turned a new page."

"I don't think I said all of that," Olympia said.

"It was implied." Lavonda smiled because she was happy, at peace with her decision. "He's not an ax murderer, and he's promised to answer any of my questions. He's also back on track with his research."

"Certainly sounds like a good way to move forward. Enjoy yourself and remember to double check the...you know."

"You know?"

"You *know*." Olympia's voice dropped to a whisper. "The nighttime protection."

"It seems to me that failed protection is exactly how baby Audie came to be."

"That was fate intervening and it hasn't worked out so bad."

For a millisecond, Lavonda imagined a redheaded baby with freckles and then shut that down. "I'm going to the drugstore as soon as I'm off the phone." Olympia was still laughing when Lavonda hung up.

JONES SPENT THE afternoon in the barn grooming the horses, moving feed, chasing Cat away from his feet and finally talking with Reese as he cleaned out the little animal's stall. Not that it needed it. Lavonda took care of the animals each morning. After the confrontation in the president's office, he'd known she wouldn't appreciate him even suggesting that he'd help her.

"Laddie," Jones said to Reese in the broadest accent he could muster. "Are ye ready for an adventure?"

Reese stared straight at him, a piece of hay hanging from his mouth, obviously not impressed or interested in Jones's comments.

"Ready or not, we'll be leaving tomorrow," he continued in his usual voice. "I believe that Lavonda may have deliberately forgotten to get us Hobnobs, until I reminded her."

"Yee-owl." Cat came running, belly swinging.

"Dear Lord. How did she hear me say that? When I can saddle you up and ride you, then you'll have earned a biscuit."

Despite her bulk, Cat easily leaped into the stall and settled herself onto Reese's back. The little burro dropped his head and dozed off.

"I thought creatures were open to conversation with humans." That was in the movies. This was real life, where he'd placed himself into a position that meant he needed to forget about Lavonda and anything that had happened between them. "The best-case scenario is that I find the cache, then everyone will forgive me for everything. Right, Reese?" The donkey didn't twitch. Cat lifted her lip and showed a canine.

He couldn't delay further. He needed to organize his supplies and equipment because he had to go back to the desert to finish his research. He had to turn something in about beans *and* find the cache.

He knew he was close to finding where his relative had noted his first clue.

Jones made his way from the barn to the ranch house, walking slowly in the heat. He wished he had his lucky straw hat—that was gone, like a lot of things in his life. He'd have to make do with the replacement he'd found in town and hope his luck hadn't run out when he'd lost the original in the arroyo.

"Jones," Lavonda shouted as he set foot in the kitchen.

Damn.

"I need to talk to you."

He'd bet she did. He didn't need her telling him again that he was a lying sack of—

"Yo, cowboy," she said. "Didn't you hear me? I want to talk about the next trip. Get a drink and we'll sit on the patio." She walked off.

He grabbed the iced tea he was coming to enjoy and followed her outside.

"Not too bad for early summer." She sipped her own drink and stared at the glass. "While I'm not happy about you hiding your name. I also understand that we all want a fresh start. After all, that's probably why half of the settlers ended up in Arizona. You still owe the university their bean paper. I've talked to Gwen to re-confirm the university is okay with me remaining as your guide. She agreed that it would expedite the process but made clear the university would not ask me to take you into the desert. I'm okay with that and I've got nothing on my plate for the next month. That's enough time, right?"

"Bean paper?"

"Whatever." She waved a hand. "I was asking about the timing."

"A month should be adequate." Had she said she'd forgiven him? And if so, what did that mean? "We're good then?" She cocked her head to one side. "I'm forgiven?"

"Nothing to forgive. But do you really go by Ross?"

"Only on paper. My family and colleagues call me Jones."

"I always wanted a nickname."

"You did?"

"I hated my name. For six months, I made everyone call me Lizzie. That ended when my brother, Danny, got me an ax."

Jones knew that that this was significant but for the life of him he couldn't figure out why.

"You know, Lizzie Borden took an ax, and gave her parents forty whacks?"

"Is that a nursery rhyme?"

"Not really. A famous nineteenth-century accused murderess. Anyway, I gave up on the name change." She took another long swallow of iced tea. "I'm going to the store before we hit the trail. Do you need anything? More Hobnobs?"

"Yes, please," he said. "I had hoped to leave tomorrow."

"Day after will have to do."

He nodded. "You're sure? I would understand if you changed your mind."

"Yes."

He watched her fiddle with the glass. "Is this just a professional trip?"

Her wide-eyed gaze caught his, then she looked back down. "It might be best."

"Maybe."

"It's not like you're staying in Arizona."

They would have to break it off sooner or later. Maybe sooner was better. But, damn, he wasn't quite ready for what they had to end. He probably should just be happy that she was still speaking to him. Yeah. That's all he could hope for. "I'll work on the maps and coordinates."

"Good idea."

LAVONDA SETTLED INTO the tent despite the stifling warmth. She needed to be by herself, away from Jones after two long days on the trail. She lay back and stared at the smooth nylon in cheery yellow, willing the tears away. She'd always known her time with Jones had an end date. She closed her eyes. *Lavonda, my love.* Her eyes popped open. He'd said that in the heat of passion, before she'd found out that he was Jones but not Jones, that he was after beans but not beans. He'd probably said it to hundreds of lassies. She was going to go to sleep. She would not think of Jones. She would not think about what it would be like at the ranch without him, until she found her next job and revived her own career. It would be better. No more worries on where Cat hung out. No more driving an extra thirty minutes to buy Hobnobs.

She sat up, lit the lantern and dug until she found her pen and paper. Tonight called for a pro and con list.

"Everything okay?" Jones asked from outside her tent.

Her pen skittered across the paper. "Can't a woman turn on a light?"

"I thought you were asleep."

Was his voice closer? "Trying. It's—" She'd nearly said hot, but her mind filled in, *That's what she said.* Her heart broke a little. "Making notes on my career plan." *Liar.*

"I'm certain that you'll have no difficulties finding a job. I could give you a reference."

"I'm good." Inside, she yelled, *Go away.* She swore she could smell him through the thin tent material.

"Fine. Just offering to help."

"Stop talking. That would be a help."

He didn't respond. Had rudeness worked? She listened for his footsteps—no one could sneak around in boots. Nothing. "Jones? What are you doing?" She made a bargain with herself. If he didn't answer by the time she counted to eight, then she was throwing back the tent flap and giving him what for. *One. Two. Three. Four.*

"Shite," he said, so softly that she almost couldn't hear him.

"Will you stop skulking around out there? It's kind of creepy."

"I do not skulk."

"Then what are you doing?" She might just peek to check on him.

"I'm…stretching."

"For goodness' sake," Lavonda said at the same time she threw back the tent flap. She couldn't sleep or work with him looming outside. "Stretch somewhere else."

"That's what she said?"

"You're never going to get that right."

"I know. It's just that. Hell," he breathed out, and turned from her. "I'm trying to be a professional."

"A professional what?"

"No more lies, right? I want to make love to you."

"Oh."

"That's what she said, and I'll not hear that I didn't get it right," he said, rolling every one of the *r*'s.

Just before she completely gave in to her shivers of delight, Lavonda thought to herself that a kilted cowboy might just be the kind of cowboy she could love.

Chapter Eleven

As a child, Jones had dreamed about being in the desert by a campfire, as he'd seen in films. The reality had turned out to be a one-burner camp stove and dehydrated meals. No cookie in a wagon making meals of biscuits and stew and no glow of oil lanterns—solar-powered halogen lamps lit up the site. Still, being in Arizona had lived up to his imaginings in many ways and surpassed his expectation in others.

He glanced at Lavonda as she carefully ate a spoonful of the nondescript food. They'd go their separate ways in another three weeks, unless he found the cache sooner. His heart squeezed. Excitement for what his future would hold when he found a cave filled with gold, silver and relics. Right, that's what it was. He'd be set at the university. No one would think of him as Iain's younger, less talented, slightly mad brother, discoverer of the Dolly-Acropolis. He might even be able to convince a university in Arizona to take him on. The sand and heat of the desert felt right, as if they were his destiny. He snorted.

"What?" Lavonda asked. "Channeling your inner Reese?" On cue, the little burro gave a matching snort. She laughed. He smiled.

"I was thinking about the biscuits and stew you always see cowboys eating in the films. This is certainly not that."

"Nope. Sweet-and-sour pork. Not the worst."

"Damned by faint praise."

She shrugged. "We've got Hobnobs, cowboy." Reese brayed and shifted where he was staked out. His horse companions barely lifted their heads. They were used to the overly dramatic donkey.

"That almost makes up for the lack of biscuits."

"That's not true. Hobnobs are biscuits."

"Very funny. I've become thoroughly American and the only biscuits I acknowledge are a mile high, fluffy and slathered with jam."

"We'll stop at the diner in Angel Crossing on the way home. No need to beg."

"What are you talking about?"

"You're hankering for biscuits, and the diner should have them because it's a diner."

"Hankering?"

"I'm working on giving you the proper cowboy adventure. I wouldn't want it to be said that the Angel Crossing campus had not provided its visitors with a superior desert experience."

Suddenly, he didn't want the lighthearted banter. "I'm not certain I'm going back to Scotland."

"Really. Do you have other digs planned?" Lavonda didn't look up from her food.

"Not yet." The more he thought about it, the more sense it made to leverage the cache into a position at a US university.

"I didn't realize beans were such a big thing."

"Agriculture, really. It's an important branch."

Important, but boring. He'd finally admitted it. He couldn't care less about beans or wheat or anything else he'd studied.

"Farming is still important. I mean, how else would we have these superior freeze-dried meals?"

"You know, I wanted to be a cowboy."

"What little boy doesn't?"

"In Scotland. When your family have been academics since before the Rising?"

"You can't be a scholar and a cowboy? We have cowboy poets and singing cowboys."

"You know about my relative—the cousin a couple times removed—who explored the West." Should he be traveling over this dangerous ground? She wouldn't guess he hadn't given up his search from a little talk.

"Where'd he settle?" She put down her packet of "food" and looked at him with the wide-eyed stare that made him want to…well, he wasn't sure what, except he didn't want to hide anything from her. What else could he do, though?

"Nevada or Utah, I think, to work for a university studying the ancient sites."

"He studied indigenous culture way back when?"

Jones shrugged and his shoulder pulled a little, a reminder of his adventure with Reese. Is that how it would feel when he left Lavonda? A twinge? The only reminder an ache from time to time. He feared that it would be something much more painful and sharp. "He looked for links between the peoples of the Americas and the East. An unusual line of inquiry."

"That's a new one. Although there were those land bridges, right? That allowed people to populate all of the continents. I can watch a public television series with the best of them. Did he find any links?"

Should he reveal everything? Maybe she'd already found it online anyway. "He reportedly found obviously not Native American and possibly Mongol cultural items in materials being taken to the missions."

"I can't believe I never heard about that, but I guess that's why you were looking for it? None of the materials made it to the university or a museum. That's odd."

"Yes, odd, and ancient history..." *Nice way to redirect the conversation, Jones.* "What about you? What are you going to do when you no longer have to follow a bean researcher into the desert?"

"First, I have to write a scintillating article about said research and another piece about the petroglyphs and their preservation. After that, I'll be looking for a job. A real job."

"This isn't a real job?"

She shook her head, her smooth hair moving gently. "I can't pretend anymore that it is. You know I was in corporate communications." She didn't wait for answer. "I was good at it. I'm not bragging—I was. But I burned out. My company had been bought out and I fell on the sword so another person in my department could keep her job during the downsizing. I've kept busy, helping my sister and a friend. Then Gwen called and I came here. I imagined I could go back to being a cowgirl, but you know, you never can go home again."

"Corporate communications. That's what you really want to do?" He'd had the feeling that she'd been dissatisfied with her life in a vague way. As if he could figure out these sorts of emotional puzzles.

Pottery shards were about the only puzzle he was competent to solve.

"It's what I do, and what I do well. I love the West and even loved the rodeo, but it felt so…small."

He laughed, then he realized she wasn't joking. "What do you mean 'small'? The Highlands are big, open spaces, I'll grant you. But nothing like this. Everything is farther and bigger. Even the sunsets are brighter and more colorful."

"That's just pollution. The rodeo was small because, even though we traveled, we saw the same people and we did the same thing every week. Then, of course, there was the fact that my two siblings were very, very good at what they did."

"Weren't you a champion?"

"That was years ago, and my heart wasn't in it like Jessie's and Danny's." She paused for barely a moment and if he hadn't known her so well he might not have noticed. She went on brightly, "I've had a good, long break—like a professor's sabbatical, since the last 'realignment of assets.' Businesses should probably allow employees to do that periodically, without the downsizing. I know when I go back to work, I'll be better."

Maybe he didn't have the skills to put together her "shards," but he couldn't help himself. She wanted something to call her own. He could understand that. He fought for that all the time as he tried to make his own mark, which had led to the dolls and now had him on the path to Kincaid's Cache. "During sabbaticals, professors work on research or writing for publication."

"Oh, then maybe just a gap year?"

"So you've had your gap year—"

"More like two years."

"Two years, then. You're ready to go back to your corporate job, all refreshed."

"Sure."

Another shard in the puzzle, explaining what she didn't want. So what did she want? "That wasn't very enthusiastic."

"Long day," she said, getting up from her seat. "I'll throw away your packet of dinner—love those kind of dishes—and get the Hobnobs."

Too many missing shards for him to understand what was going on. What did he want it to be? For all of her pieces to fit together so they could recapture the joy they'd found in each other's arms. The recent desperate edge to their lovemaking worried him. Exactly, though, who was the most desperate?

"Hobnobs, sir. Coffee?"

He tugged on her arm and she fell into his lap. "Whether you're a cowgirl or a be-suited—"

"That's not a word," she said, pushing against him.

"It is if I say it is. I was trying to pay you a compliment. I know that no matter what you put your mind to do, you will do it well, with integrity and panache."

"Really?"

He didn't know where to put that shard, so he kissed her, because that's when everything made the most sense.

She moved her lips away enough to say to him, "I could say the same thing about you, but you've got swagger, not panache."

"That's what she said."

LAVONDA HEARD HER siblings before she saw them in the downtown Tucson restaurant, one of those old-fashioned, been-around-forever cantinas. Jessie had organized the meet-up. Lavonda had been happy for the excuse to be away from the ranch and Jones after returning from their latest foray into the desert. She'd promised herself that when they got back to Hacienda Bunuelos she'd get serious about rebooting her career. Her great contribution to that plan was posting her résumé on a PR job site.

"Hi, everyone," she said when she walked up to the table. Seated were Jessie and Payson and his brother, Spence, and his wife, Olympia, and, of course, her own little brother, Danny, who topped all of them at six-three.

"Finally," Jessie said. "We figured you'd have some excuse to cancel, like you were leading another bean safari."

"It wasn't—"

"I'm starved," Danny said. "Less talking, more ordering."

The conversation moved to food and details about caring for babies. Lavonda had forgotten how nice it was to hang out with her family. Mama and Daddy were the only pieces missing, but they were traveling around the state visiting rodeo friends.

"Quiet," Jessie said after the plates were taken away and before dessert arrived. "Payson and I want to—"

Danny raised his beer and said, "Remind everyone how much they love each other."

"Shut up, Danny," Jessie said without heat as she stood. "You're just jealous. I—"

Her sister choked up and tears shone in her eyes. Triple crap. Something big and bad had happened. Jessie never cried. Both she and Olympia leaped from their seats to go to her. "What? What's wrong?"

Jessie shook her head and gave a trembling smile. "It's all good." Then Payson stood behind his wife, his expression heartbreakingly tender as his arm held her and his hand went to her belly.

"You're pregnant," Olympia and Lavonda yelled at the same time.

Lavonda barely heard what anyone else said as she grabbed and hugged her sobbing sister, who murmured, "It's just the hormones."

Jessie and Payson had been trying to get pregnant since they got married for the second time. It had been particularly hard on her when Olympia had been pregnant last year. Now, Jessie and her husband glowed with happiness. Lavonda was thrilled for her sister, but a little tug around her heart reminded her that she was alone. Like Danny, but not like him, because he was a hound dog to beat all hound dogs, with a different buckle bunny every night. He never seemed to want or need more. Back before her "gap years," as she was beginning to think of her time away from her real work, she'd been happy with her job and her well-organized dates. It had never gotten serious because neither she nor her boyfriends had had the time for a relationship or one of them was moving to another job, up another rung.

"Here," Payson said as he handed her a glass. "Those of us not pregnant are toasting." He laughed. The serious surgeon who had the focus of a rattlesnake about to bite looked and sounded happier than she'd ever seen him.

Lavonda wanted Jones to be here with her. She wanted his big strong arms around her. She wanted to be enveloped in his familiar scent of pine and moss. She wanted all of that—and shouldn't. What they had wasn't permanent like Jessie and Payson or Olympia and Spence.

She felt the heavy weight of Danny's arm across her shoulder. "Drink up and celebrate," he said. "'Cause it's better them than us, right?"

"At least it will mean that Mama will stop bugging us about grandbabies." She forced out a laugh.

"There is that. You and me should go out on the town."

"In Angel Crossing? What would that be, a beer at the *one* bar? Besides, I've got commitments at the ranch and with the university."

He looked at her hard and said seriously, "If you need me to give him a bloody nose, just let me know." Danny gave her a brotherly one-armed squeeze, then went to talk with Payson and Spence.

She glanced at Olympia. Had she told him about Jones? And if he knew, then Jessie knew. She'd talk with them about it later. Tonight was Jessie's. Lavonda was going to focus on her sister and the miracle of another baby.

When they left the restaurant, Danny followed her to her car and said again, "We should hang out."

"I'll call."

"Really. I'd like to show you around the town. It's one of those places that just needs… I may need…" He stopped himself and gave her one of his slow grins that always made all of her friends sigh, until he acted more tomcat than lap-cat. "I've got plans that you might be able to help me with."

"Just let me know." Danny had never asked for help before. In fact, he'd always told his sisters to leave him alone, because he already had a mama, thank you very much.

He hugged her hard again. "You call if you need me to come out and kick his ass."

"I don't know what you're talking about."

"I'm your brother. Don't BS me. Plus, you know that Olympia has already told me all about the guy in the kilt. Doesn't sound like much of a cowboy, but if you—"

"There's nothing."

"Doesn't appear that way to me."

"Like you're an expert on relationships. What has your longest been? Three months?"

"We're not talking about me."

"We are when you're trying to tell me what to do. Plus, you're the baby brother—you don't get to do that."

"I do when my big sister is getting up close and personal with a guy in a kilt and cowboy hat who's on his way back to wherever he came from any day now."

"It's all good."

"'Don't serve me bull crap and call it pâté,' as Mama would say."

Lavonda laughed, proof to herself and Danny everything really was fine.

"I won't say I told you so or anything else if you give me a call. Okay?" She nodded and let Danny open the door to her Mini Cooper. "When are you going to get a real car?"

"As soon as I grow another foot," she answered as she always did. She waved as she pulled out of the lot. The familiarity of the banter should have made her feel comfortable, like settling back into a pillow. Instead, it opened the ache in her heart. A temporary one. As soon as the Scot went back to the Highlands, she'd be happy and on her way to another corporate high-rise, spinning into gold the latest disaster or discovery.

While she did that spinning, she'd get the cash to buy the ranch. She'd talk to Gwen about that. Could she keep her feet firmly in both lives? The ranch being home and her work...her work? When had being a guru of corporate communications become just work? When she'd burned out from one too many news cycles and "rightsizings." She'd been good at her job and committed to each company. She'd climbed up the ladder, getting nearer to the coveted corner office. She'd happily wiped the desert dust from her boots and put away the fantasy of settling for a cowboy. She'd wanted something else. She'd wanted to know what life was like beyond the arena. The trouble was the corporate cowboys didn't understand the rules. They bent and broke them and expected her to fix it all. That's what she'd tried to do her whole life. Fix things, people and animals. Could she fix herself? Or, maybe, she didn't need fixing?

Crap. She'd missed the turnoff for the ranch. She swung around and back onto the long drive. She stopped in the middle of the dirt track. No one else would be coming this way. She turned off the Mini and got out to walk in the dust. Crappedy crap. Had she just spent the past eight years of her life proving to no one that she wasn't a cowgirl and was a success because she wore a suit to work every day? She couldn't have been that shallow. Could she? Had she been embarrassed by her family and her rodeo life because it didn't include Chanel and Coach? Worse. She'd imagined that if she was a success and could fix everyone's lives by buying those things they'd always wanted, then everyone would love her. Exactly how well had that worked? Well enough that she burned out, drifted through her life for nearly two years and now was thinking about doing it all again. Idiot.

No. Not an idiot. Just a cowgirl who'd grabbed the wrong end of the bull.

She stopped walking and looked up at the dark sky. She really was good at PR. Look what she'd done for Jessie's therapy program. With her help, she'd gotten enough notice in the right places for Hope's Ride to be on its way to success. Maybe she and her job hadn't been shallow and meaningless. What did that mean for her now? The ranch had become home, hadn't it? Did that mean she needed to return to being a cowgirl, to riding, mucking stables and breaking in horses? Or did Hacienda Bunuelos feel like home because of Jones? Her thoughts skittered away from that conclusion. She couldn't solve any of this tonight. She still was obliged to lead the Scotsman into the desert. Piece of cake. She'd ridden bronc with a broken wrist. This couldn't be any more painful.

Chapter Twelve

Lavonda looked at the list on the laptop's screen and wondered when the universe had found such a great sense of humor. Just as she'd convinced herself that staying in Arizona was exactly what she wanted, a position she'd applied for right after her downsizing had come open again. They wanted to talk to her about it, so saying yes should've been a no-brainer, except the job was in Hong Kong. She'd always looked at companies that would take her as far from Arizona as possible. Plus, this company and the description of the position had checked off every one of her must-haves on the list she'd made after her second corporate job.

To clarify the challenges and assets, as she'd been taught, of this potential job she'd been making a pro and con list, just like she'd done hundreds of times before, from how to tell Mama and Daddy she would be a corporate executive, not a rodeo queen, to how to make a chemical spill sound like a positive thing. So far, for the pros she had:

1. Living in Hong Kong.
2. Making big money.

The con side had grown to fifteen items.

Of course, the big money might be the biggest pro, maybe the only one that counted if it meant she could seriously consider buying Hacienda Bunuelos as her...well, as her second home. She still hadn't figured out exactly how the ranch fit into her future, only that it needed to. She had to come up with more pros. Money couldn't trump all. She'd tried that before and been miserable.

3. Real Chinese food.

That was lame. She'd reached the bottom of the barrel if that was a pro. She opened another document on her screen, hoping a change in work would jar loose more ideas. This spreadsheet was familiar. It mapped out how she would restore Jones's reputation, if he asked her, which he hadn't. On the other hand, he was a guy and more cowboy than his kilt implied. Asking for help didn't show up on his list of the best ways to address a problem.

"Do you have a—" Jones's voice sounded behind her.

She jumped and squeaked out a girlie scream.

"Sorry," he said hastily. "I thought you had heard me come in. Cat yowled."

She dropped her hand from her racing heart. She saw Cat twining around his legs. "I was working."

"Ah," he answered with a knowing hum. He loomed behind her. She ignored the heat that flushed through her when she caught his pine-and-moss scent. "What is this? Lavonda—"

"It's what I do. I can't help it if my mind is just a PR machine."

"You haven't done any of this, have you?" He gestured to the laptop's screen.

"They're just ideas."

"Not very good ones, especially when I didn't ask for any of it."

She'd treat him like one of the big bosses who were all ego and little logic. Managing them took finesse and saying yes without saying yes. "This was an academic exercise. Practice for when I get back to my 'real' work."

"Bloody hell," Jones muttered. "You don't understand. Glasgow called and…my visa is being cut off early because of my 'breach of academic ethics.' In other words, I'm getting the boot and I'll need to leave right away."

"You can't leave," she blurted out, hearing the desperate edge to her voice. "You have to fight this."

"The paperwork is in process. Thank you for your hospitality and help on the trail." He thrust out his hand.

Wait? This was goodbye and he'd just thanked her for her "hospitality"? She sucked in a breath to stop herself from spewing out something that she'd have to fix later. "You're not leaving right now, are you?"

He turned away and said, "I've got to return to Scotland as soon as we complete our next trip. I got them to give me that much time."

"I can't imagine Gwen doesn't have a say in you leaving the country before your bean research is complete."

He walked out of the room.

She panicked. All her plans fled and the only thought looping through her brain was that Jones was leaving forever. She couldn't let him do that. It would tank his career. Her plan for him could still work. She just had to persuade Gwen and the university to convince his school in Glasgow to give him more time. Her mind had started working again.

While she worked on that, there also had to be some kind of legal delay, right? There was always a legal solution. She called Spence, sure he'd know what to do to help Jones.

"Hello, Lavonda. You're calling to take Calvin and Audie for two weeks, right? Then Olympia and I are going to—"

"Only if you find a way to keep the professor here in the States. His visa is being pulled and then he'll have to leave. He's nearly done with his research. If he doesn't get that done and write an article, then who knows what will happen to him." She'd made up a lot of that, although she thought she'd guessed pretty well. "Spence?"

"I'm thinking."

"I don't have a lot of time. The visa—"

"That's the easy part to fix. You can do like Olympia and I did. Go to Vegas, get married. I did it to keep custody of Calvin, but it would work as well for the Scotsman to get his US status instantly—nearly instantly."

Why hadn't she thought of that? They could be in Vegas in hours, get married and then she'd have plenty of time to solve the problem of his career.

"Lavonda, I was kidding. Olympia and I were in a totally different situation. We weren't trying to fool the feds with our quickie wedding. And let me tell you, immigration takes everything very seriously."

She waved a hand that Spence couldn't see, because she wanted him to be quiet while she analyzed the possibility. "We could marry. He'd stay. Finish his research so he'd get the evidence he needed to write the paper, which will fulfill his grant and then they'll have to keep him. The paper equals his job. I could put off going to Hong Kong until—"

"Hong Kong? What's in Hong Kong?"

Crappedy crap. She hadn't meant to let that cat out of the bag. What was wrong with her? Her entire career had been built on her ability to keep her mouth shut when needed. "This could work, Spence. Thanks." She hung up before he could say more. She started a new document to outline the Green Card Marriage Plan.

Cat yowled as she sauntered in. "What?" The feline rushed over to her and bumped her head against Lavonda's leg. "You agree this is a good plan. You're doing it for the Hobnobs. Unlike me. I'm doing it for the good of the archaeological community." Cat sat back and stared. "For archaeology and beans." The unblinking blue eyes bored into her brain. How? She was a cat. "This has nothing to do with making him stay in Arizona. I'm only doing this to help him stay in the States to reboot his career. He doesn't deserve to have it messed up again because of a few little snafus."

Marrying him would be no big deal, just like signing a noncompete agreement. Any fluttering in her stomach related directly to her plan to live in Hong Kong. After all, she'd get to have real Chinese food every day.

As LAVONDA AND JONES rode farther on their hastily organized final trek, her mind drifted from guiding the horse through the increasingly dense scrub to her plan. The one where she used her PR skills to convince her employer that she would go to Hong Kong later—if the company ever called back. She'd stay in the States until he finished his research and—voilà—career saved.

She urged Brownie forward. The horse didn't like the switched-up schedule, where they explored early in the morning and the twilight to avoid the worst of the heat, now that summer had come to the desert. The heat of the day was for lying low, which had come to mean time alone together for Lavonda and Jones. She'd tried to tell herself to stick to her own tent, but then she'd catch his mossy scent or hear him talking with Reese and she couldn't resist him. Didn't want to resist him.

She shook off her worry. What had she learned riding those broncs? Hang on for eight seconds and give the judges a show. Pay attention to what was happening now, not what might happen tomorrow or the next second, but what was happening right now. That's what she had to do. Hang on to the time they had and not worry too much about would happen next. Could she do that, though?

Jones, on Joe, walked in front of her, head down and staring at his phone or whatever electronic equipment he held in his large hand. The sun caught the tips of hair that curled under the band of his new lucky hat, nearly identical to the one he'd gotten at the Old West section of Edinburgh. He'd promised to show her the street. That would never happen.

Hang on for eight seconds.

She scanned the horizon. Their goal—which she

should be focused on—was an arched cat. They'd stopped three times to investigate formations that, with some imagination, could have been cats. Lavonda couldn't imagine that ancient settlements were so difficult to find if they'd been found before.

BROWNIE STOPPED TO nose at a bush. Lavonda let him rest while she scanned the horizon for shade and/or water to make a daytime camp. She looked behind her at Reese, head down and drowsing. No water nearby or he would have been prick-eared and bright-eyed. She looked to the east, into the sun. Crappedy crap.

"Jones," she shouted. "Two o'clock."

He didn't stop Joe.

"Jones," she yelled again. "Two o'clock. It's the cat."

His hat moved, and she knew he squinted against the sun to see what she had. He pointed the piece of electronics that way. "It's a bit off the numbers."

"Worth a check, don't you think?"

"We've thought the same thing before. It's probably another dead end. That's the way it is in archaeology."

"It could be the real deal, too. Come on, cowboy. Draggin' your boots won't make it any less the right or wrong place."

"Wait," he said, putting his hand out to stop her as her horse and the little donkey tried to pass. Both Brownie and Reese were unimpressed, sidling away.

"Watch it."

"Sorry, but I need to say something." He pushed the hat back and the crease on his forehead and the sweaty bangs touched something deep in her.

"Shoot." She loosened her grip on the reins to keep the horse from feeling the sudden tension that raced through her.

"I don't know how to say this—"

He broke off and her heart sank, because suddenly she knew. There was another lie. He wouldn't look her in the eye. He was married. He had a girlfriend. Oh, crap. She knew that she shouldn't have trusted him. She knew he wasn't a real cowboy, the kind of man who told the truth no matter the consequences.

"You ass. You've got a woman back in Scotland." She pulled the horse's head around to take off. Brownie snorted and danced. What the hell was she doing? You didn't treat your mount like that. And exactly what was she going to do—race away? Not likely through the boulders and scrub. She pulled in a breath.

"Hell, Lavonda, why would you think I would... I never would... How could you even imagine that I would do anything like that?"

"What else would you lie about?"

"Actually, it's about what we've been looking for."

"Beans. You agreed to complete your research." This was beginning to make a sick sense.

"Yes, well." Jones adjusted his seat and Joe gave him a look over his shoulder. Jones absently patted the gelding. "I told you before the beans won't restore my reputation or get me the chairmanship."

"This time you deserve whatever the university throws at you. You know the 'fool me once, shame on you'? Well, you've fooled me twice and it's still shame on you. If I didn't think you'd die on your own, I'd leave you out here in the desert."

DAMN, THAT HURT. She'd reacted worse than he'd hoped. Maybe he should've stuck with his original plan, which was to wait until they'd actually found the cache to give her a full explanation of what had been going on. Then today, the way the sun sparked off her hair while she sang off-key to the horses, it had hit him. She wasn't an assistant or a colleague or whatever else he'd been convincing himself she was. She was Lavonda—the woman that he…liked…cared for but certainly didn't love. As such, she deserved to know what he was doing.

"Let's go," she said, aiming her horse at the cat formation.

He wanted her to understand that he didn't have a choice. He'd had to do this all under the radar for very good and very logical reasons. "Lavonda, let me explain."

Brownie stopped and Lavonda whipped her head around, her flat-crowned hat shading her face so he couldn't see her expression. "Don't. Just don't."

He had brains to spare. He shut up.

The stones really did look like an arched cat. Could it be what the American Kincaid, his much-removed cousin, had described? And wouldn't that be the final straw or bead in his never-ending string of bad luck. When he made his greatest discovery, he lost the respect of the woman that he…liked.

The horses and Reese picked their careful way across the steeply sloped terrain. On other days of the trek, they would have made camp to rest in the heat and…they would have made love. By unspoken agreement, they didn't stop today, eating in the saddle and allowing the horses to finally rest when they had gone as far as was safe on horseback. Lavonda and Jones scrambled their way up the remainder of the slope to a stack of rocks that had obviously been piled into the shape of a cat.

"Wait," Jones said, touching Lavonda's arm. She pulled away immediately. "You wouldn't allow me to explain myself earlier, but please allow me the courtesy now."

She nodded tightly. "Quick. It's hot."

This was worse than any oral exam. Worse than facing his brother and the full department after Dolly-Acropolis. He'd been formulating this speech for Lavonda for the past hour. Not one word had stuck. "After the dolls—"

"Which you lied about."

"I didn't... You're right—I lied about it. It was embarrassing. Worse. It tanked my career. What I'd been working toward since I was in grammar school. My brother always got firsts and taunted me for years about my interest in the West, no matter that the Kincaid family had ties there. If I wanted to be taken seriously as an archaeologist then I needed to study in Scotland or on the Continent. My brother and my father had a very stern talk with me in my second year at university, after I'd suggested a research project in Arizona. They made it clear that I wouldn't finish the program and would never get a job if I continued my pursuits. They were right, but I did at least choose my own field—agriculture."

"We're burning daylight," she said, but a hint of interest had entered her voice.

"I was lucky enough to get connected with a researcher in Iceland and traveled there for digs nearly every summer. I got really good at riding their po-nies…horses. Have you seen them? Tough little bug-gers. Something like Reese…only bigger, with more hair…maybe not like Reese, after all."

"Ticktock, doc."

"I'd begun to make a name for myself in Iceland, looking at the use of grains and legumes in early set-tlers, when the chairmanship came open. It was be-tween me and Iain. They chose him, but it had been made clear to me that if I could make a discovery that was original and significant, I would be considered during the next round. All that stood between me and finally being able to do the research that I wanted, finally being out from under Iain's shadow, was one good piece of archaeology. I got a lead based on what I thought was a believable oral story about Viking gold… You know the rest."

"I'm supposed to believe that?"

"I wish you would."

"If wishes were horses, ponies would ride."

"That really doesn't make any sense."

"You had your say. We'll check this out because we've come this far, then we're heading back to the ranch."

He'd tried. Time to focus on what was important. Really important. Finding Kincaid's Cache. He stared at the obviously man-made cat sculpture. He looked at the larger formation and then the smaller one. There had been that article about the original cave attrib-uted to his relative being filled with Egyptian trea-sure and Egyptians worshipped cats.

He strolled around the pedestal of the cat, then there it was, plain as day or the nose on Mount Rushmore. The symbol Kincaid had used to indicate the treasure. Jones took in a long breath, then settled into viewing the rocks like the scientist he was. More symbols with the same pattern as those in the journal—definitely faint but still visible on the lee side of the rocks, more than one hundred years after Kincaid had etched them there. He matched the symbols to the key he had memorized. The cave wasn't here and the directions said to—

"What did you find?"

What to tell Lavonda? This could be another dead end. Another Dolly-Acropolis. "The journals were in code and this cat has clues."

"Code? Really."

"Here." He pulled her to the side of the cat with engravings. He pointed to the first shape. "That's what he used to indicate the treasure."

"Treasure? What are we, ten?"

"His words, not mine. The other symbols explain the exact location of the cave or chest—he used the words interchangeably."

"Where does it tell you to go? And you'd better not give me some hooey about where the bear of Hopi plays with the hare of Zuni."

"The American Kincaid was an archaeologist and scientist, too. The code was because of the value of his find. The symbols give me coordinates."

"He just couldn't have put the actual coordinates in the journal." Lavonda started to turn away.

"He insisted that other archaeologists as well as the US government were after the materials. He didn't want to put every detail in one place."

"Baby Jesus and his halo of angels. We'll go to the

coordinates, but that's as far as I, the horses and Reese are going. If the treasure isn't there, we're heading back to the ranch. I can't put myself in any more jeopardy with the university. I should probably have called Gwen as soon as you told me what you were doing."

Chapter Thirteen

Lavonda forced herself to stay quiet and not step in to spin Jones's confession. She'd told him when they'd gotten back to the ranch that either he told the university what he'd been doing instead of his *real* research—again—or she would do it. He'd stepped up.

Of course, the coded message on the cat hadn't led them to a cave of gold. Surprise, surprise. Instead, it had ended at another stack of stones—this one in the shape of a pyramid—with another coded message. Lavonda had stuck to her guns and told Jones they were returning to home base. He'd capitulated after another fervent speech. She'd nearly caved—no pun intended—but then she'd imagined another crawl across the TV screen: Archaeologist from Angel Crossing Campus Dies in Search for Buried Treasure. Not the kind of publicity Gwen wanted.

While she hadn't changed her mind on heading back to the ranch, she had agreed with at least a part of his speech. If he had found materials he said the American Kincaid had hidden, then his career would be made. He could lecture around the world, teach wherever he wanted, including Arizona, as well as secure TV appearances, book deals and funding for whatever he wanted to research. The find would have boosted the prestige of Gwen's small branch campus, too.

Lavonda was brought back abruptly to Stanley's windowless and messy office.

"You said that you would continue with your proposed research," the older professor said with a snap.

"I went to sites in my proposal and noted the use of beans. At the same time, I used the journal to find Kincaid's markers for his cache."

Stanley shook his head. "This is beyond unprofessional."

"Any research beyond that outlined in my proposal was done on my own. No one knew what I was doing."

"Not even your brother? Chair of the department? Am I supposed to believe that—"

"Iain does not know."

Another lie, Lavonda knew. Jones had confessed his brother had discovered the American Kincaid's—as the family called him—journals were missing. She wouldn't pile on this detail. In the end, what mattered was what Jones had done.

Stanley stared at Jones with a flinty gaze. "Your guide is a university employee. Why didn't she report this?"

Crappedy crap.

Jones jumped in, "I lied to her. She didn't know about any of it."

"I've got to call Dr. Hernandez. I'm not certain what further contractual issues we may have."

"Lavonda… Ms. Leigh didn't know anything. She only found out when I told her."

"Be that as it may, Dr. Hernandez must be involved."

"Please, Stanley, this is not her fault. I take full responsibility."

"I'm sorry."

"I'll stay to speak with Dr. Hernandez," Jones said, making it obvious that he'd do whatever it took to make Gwen understand the situation.

Her kilted cowboy, knight in shining armor. Way too many clichés in one thought. Of course, she wouldn't be facing her friend in the midst of all of this if it hadn't been for Jones. She had to remember that when everything went to crap and she got kicked off the ranch. It was all Jones's fault, no matter that he very rightly had taken all of the responsibility on his shoulders.

Her PR brain, though, had caught on to the idea. His treasure search could be turned into a positive for the branch. It'd certainly catch the public and media's attention. The kind of attention that was worth its weight in gold—ha-ha. Both she and Jones might come out of this okay.

GWEN GRASPED THE situation quickly and voiced, loudly, her concern over how Jones's actions flew in the face of the university's carefully constructed and enforced code of ethics.

"Lavonda was our representative on this expedition," Gwen said. "When she understood you were still looking for the 'treasure,' she should have contacted us immediately. I was concerned that her involvement with you might cloud her judgment. I was correct to worry."

Jones's fist clenched in his lap. "Lavonda was my guide."

"Uh-huh. And I'm the pope of Arizona." Gwen glared at both of them.

"Again, I take full responsibility."

"Good," Gwen said.

"Lavonda will retain her relationship with the university."

"Your protection will not ameliorate her culpability."

"She did not—"

"Do not protect her from these consequences."

"I'm not protecting her. I'm pointing out the facts of the situation."

"Hey, I'm here, you two," Lavonda broke in.

"You might not want to draw attention to that or the fact that the two of you have engaged in a sexual liaison."

Before Lavonda could protest, Jones said, "I don't believe that's any of your business."

"Normally, it wouldn't be, but when it affects the reputation of *my* school, it very much becomes my problem."

Stanley said, "This line of discussion is unproductive. Dr. Kincaid, you will receive a written notification that your presence at Angel Crossing campus is no longer welcome."

"Wait. You don't need to do this," Lavonda said, not quite knowing how they had gone from a slap on the wrist to the destruction of Jones's career. "I have ideas on how you might use his search."

"Now please, Dr. Kincaid," Gwen said firmly, ignoring Lavonda. "We'll need you off the property.

Security is here to take you to your office and lab to clear out personal items and then they will take your ID card. IT will meet you there to ensure that any materials on your computer remain. That material, per the agreement, belongs to the university."

Jones stood. Lavonda sat, not sure what to do. She needed to fix this. Why? He'd done the crime, he should do the time. What really had he done? Gone off on a treasure hunt, after he said he wouldn't, except he'd done the research he said he would but—

"Lavonda," Gwen said. "I know you had an inkling of what he was up to. I'm disappointed you didn't let me know."

She pulled herself together. Did she help Jones? Did she protect herself? "I didn't. We have been going to a variety of settlements."

"You've put me in a bad position."

Crappedy crap. "I *can* turn this into a positive."

"Absolutely not. If the alumni found out that… No. As long as this stays quiet, your involvement will remain unknown."

"I can write up something about the bean research and the grant, but that will be my last job. I want to give you notice I'll be taking a position with a company overseas."

"Finally, something is working out. I won't need to worry about a new caretaker because the ranch will soon be out of our hands."

"You didn't say anything about there being a buyer for the ranch?" Lavonda couldn't believe this part of her plan had fallen through.

"I'm not at liberty to talk about the ranch, but

you'll be able to remain there until your departure. I assume your departure is imminent."

Lavonda nodded, not sure what to say to this news. She couldn't even think about what it would mean for her. She ignored that to go over how she might fix his problem before she went to Hong Kong—when she got the call. He'd made boneheaded decisions. No doubt. Still, they weren't the kind that should end his career. She'd do the same thing for anyone.

A MAN OF JONES'S SIZE should not be difficult to find in the wide-open spaces around the ranch, especially a red-haired man who wasn't hiding. Or at least Lavonda didn't think he was hiding. She hadn't seen him since they'd gotten "home" four hours ago.

Reese's bray cut across the usual bird sounds of the desert. Lavonda searched the scrub for the little burro. Until Maizey the goat had time to do her thing, the corral areas remained choked with tumbleweeds. She caught a movement, then saw Jones. He had an ax and was chopping at a mesquite tree. He had his shirt off and a fine sheen of sweat glistened across his powerful shoulders. Had he put on sunscreen? *Yeah, Lavonda girl, pretend you were thinking about the welfare of his skin and not what that salty, sweaty skin tasted like when he was above you, in you.* What she should really be concentrating on was how she'd talk him into accepting her fix-it plan.

"Jones, did you put on sunscreen?" *Great way to start a conversation about his career.*

He stopped his swing midstroke, letting the ax fall to his side. "What?"

"What are you doing?" She'd circle around what

she wanted to say, like approaching a half-broke horse, slowly and stealthily.

"Clearing out this corral. You said something about that being on your list."

"The goat is supposed to take care of that." He grunted. Not the most positive response.

"I don't see a goat." He lifted the ax and made a final whack to the base of a young mesquite tree, and dragged it to a large pile of brush. She wouldn't tell him that the mesquite could stay. She knew a man who wasn't reasonable when she saw him.

"Can you take a break? There's something I want to talk over with you."

"I want to get this finished."

"First, you can't get this all cleared today and second…second, what I have to tell you could save your career."

He stood to his full height, tipped back his hat and gave her his squint. "Is that so? You have a time machine?"

"Ha-ha. I'm not Doctor Who. But I am a darned good media specialist."

"I told you before. No."

"You haven't even heard what I've come up with." Mama was right. No good deed goes unpunished. She remembered first seeing him at the Highland games with all the rippling muscle and testosterone-laden air. Then there was the impromptu gym in the barn. She'd remember the positive. Hadn't Oprah said that? "I know that you had pinned a lot on this discovery. I can help—"

"I don't want your help."

Lavonda's back stiffened and now she pulled herself up to her full height, returning his Old West squint. "Don't make it sound like I'm a…a…a serial killer."

"I'm fine."

"I have a brother and a brother-in-law. I know what that means."

"It means 'I am fine.' Right as rain, tip-top, A-Okay." He moved to an ironwood tree and the ax thumped against its base in sync with his words.

"That reassures me. I am a professional at spinning—"

"Offal into gold?"

"Something like that. But I have other ideas, too." Like telling herself that helping him would be a help for her career, too. When he found the treasure, the campus would get all kinds of press, which would be just the kind of campaign she could point to when she was negotiating her salary. See. It wasn't all about her cowboy in a kilt.

He stood up straight again, looming over the landscape. "I'm heading back to Glasgow, where I *might* still have a job, even if it's back to being the most junior lecturer and the assistant at a dig."

"Of course you'll have a job. Your brother wouldn't fire you."

"You shouldn't bet on that." He headed off to the barn, his cowboy boots thudding on the ground.

She'd follow him in a couple of minutes. He needed to cool off. Once she got him back on track, *then* she could move on. She needed closure, right? Making sure Jones's reputation was restored and that he still had a job was exactly what she needed to do to walk away from the affair and back onto the corporate ladder with no regrets.

JONES CLEANED OFF the ax, then checked on the gelding he'd begun to think of as his. He'd cooled off in more ways than one and knew he had even more to apologize for. He couldn't allow her to get mired in the muck of his career. He'd be lucky if his brother didn't have him deported from Scotland.

"We were so close to the cave, Joe. One more clue and we would have had it. But I've got to be off the property, pronto. Stanley and Dr. Hernandez made that clear."

Reese's bray echoed through the barn as a scuffle of Cat's claws passed by Jones, making Joe step back.

"Are you ready to listen to me now?" Lavonda asked, standing in the doorway, hands on hips in a warrior stance.

"I heard you. I didn't agree."

"Then you mustn't have listened well, because I am giving you a way out of this mess."

"I'm confused," he said because honestly he was. "You were the one who insisted I confess all and you had to know what would happen. Why the change of heart?"

"I never expected that they'd kick you off campus and the ranch."

"I already had to leave the country per Glasgow. I'll be moving on tomorrow." He'd find a hotel to stay at.

"I believe that the Angel Crossing campus and even your university are missing an amazing PR opportunity. A coded journal and legendary secret cave filled with treasure? How could that not garner a lot of interest?"

"It would, but not serious academic interest." She

didn't understand that part of the equation. No one outside the academic bubble did.

"You think I don't get it."

Hell. How had she read his mind? "It doesn't matter, but I thank you for your—"

"If you say 'for your hospitality,' I'm going to kick your cowboy butt."

"Then accept my apologies."

"For what? Lying, then lying again, then running away?"

Being accused of lying, he could live with—it was for a just cause—but he did not run away. He'd faced down everything after Dolly-Acropolis. He never ran. He stayed. He fought. "The US government might take exception to me staying, and my contract has been terminated. I'm not running."

"It'll take weeks to get all of that paperwork filed. You could find the treasure by then. I'm not giving up."

"*Now* you think I should look for a buried treasure?"

"That's what I've been saying. We've got the supply and the animals. One more trek. I'll shoot video, upload daily reports—"

"No video. No cameras. No reports." Another stream of internet videos he did not need. He understood why she was suggesting it, but he couldn't let her get dragged down by his failing career.

"I'm sure I can figure something out without the pics, but visual evidence of the find of the century would make it easier for them to throw tons of money and titles at you." Lavonda smiled broadly.

Her happiness hurt him, not because he wished

he felt the same way but because he was pretty sure he'd disappoint her.

She stopped smiling and asked, "What's wrong? It's a good plan." Her cartoon-princess eyes darkened with emotion and her mouth stopped smiling. He saw the determined cowgirl who'd gone eight seconds on a bronc. "I am fixing this whether you help me or not. There's the fact, too, that your find could mean all kinds of amazing press for the Angel Crossing campus, which I can leverage for more money when I get my next job."

She wasn't kidding and he knew her well enough to know she wouldn't be backing down. He couldn't let her throw everything into this project without giving as much as she was. "I want you to be certain. This could end badly."

"Why don't we wait to assume the worst until it happens? Plus, I've got contingencies."

He nodded. He couldn't voice both his hope and his fear. Kincaid's Cache could get him back into the good graces of his family and the university. *That's* what mattered now...and telling Lavonda the truth from here on out. *Ergo, you will be telling her that you care for her and may even love her*, the quiet voice in his head told him. The kilt-wearing, caber-tossing Jones told that little voice to shut its gob.

"Great. Get your gear packed. We're leaving at the butt-crack of dawn tomorrow." She laughed. "You'll see. It'll all work out for the best."

He watched the doorway long after she had walked through it and didn't move until Joe nibbled on the ends of his hair. He gently pushed away the gelding.

No matter what happened with this final search, he'd have the satisfaction and the memory that he'd done what he needed to do, not only for himself but also for Lavonda. He had gotten the feeling that the cave and its treasure had become just as important to her.

Chapter Fourteen

"Are you sure?" Jones asked Lavonda again, because her pupils had dilated so much her eyes looked black, a mixture of excitement and fear as she prepared to explore the cave where he was certain the American Kincaid had hidden his hoard. He would have gone in, but his shoulders wouldn't fit. He'd tried.

"Just the same as getting in the chute. I've got the rope and I've got a light." She tapped the headlamp on her hard hat.

Before he could respond, she scrambled through the hole and into the cave. With his torch, he'd been able to see the sides but not the back wall. He watched Lavonda's feet disappear and repositioned his hands on the rope for a better grip. The other end looped around Lavonda, her lifeline if anything happened. He could reel her in like a mountain trout. She tugged on the line once, meaning he was to let out more rope for her. He did that.

Warm, moist, oaty breath rolled over him. Reese stood at his side, watching the hole carefully. "I would be in there if I could," Jones said. The donkey let out a soft bray that could have been sympathy or a complaint about the rations. Another tug. He uncoiled more rope. Sweat ran from his temples. Shite. This was worse than anything he'd done. He should just pull her back. He tightened his hands to snatch her back through the ragged entrance.

"Jones..." He heard her voice faintly from the hole. "Crap. This is... Why do you have to be so huge? You need to check this for yourself. You know that I'm not a professional." The rope went slack. She was coming back to him.

Her dear pixie face appeared in the opening, with muck smeared along her jaw and across her forehead. "It's damp. And water is coming in from somewhere." She wiggled out of the opening. He grabbed her, then let her go when she stiffened. She'd been careful since they'd hit the trail to keep physical contact to a less-than-bare minimum.

"You're okay?" He wanted to hug her to him.

She waved away the question and took his hand, her eyes wide, dark and filled with...regret?

"Maybe there's another room," she started. "We should have waited and you should have gone in."

"What did you see?"

"Nothing. It's empty."

LAVONDA WATCHED JONES toss away his half-eaten Hobnob. She could only guess what he was thinking and feeling. He'd said little since he'd seen for himself, courtesy of a video on her phone, that the cave held only two mouse skeletons and the jawbone of a snake.

While they'd made camp, he'd grunted his answers. She'd taken the hint, although she'd been sure the Hobnobs and tea would move him back to being human. That had worked as well as her words. Time to distract herself from his misery by cleaning up their meal, bedding down Reese and his horse pals, then she'd crawl in the tent, alone. She'd set her phone alarm for dawn. No reason to lengthen their stay.

"What?" Jones asked from where he sat on a flat boulder, when she came out of her tent later.

"I'm trying to decide which is worse—the heat in there or the chance of waking up with a snake or lizard walking on my head."

"No scorpions?"

She laughed before she could stop herself. He went on looking out at the desert and not her.

"As a kid, in the Highlands and on holiday, we sometimes camped rough. Well, my brother and I did."

So they weren't talking about the great big elephant-sized lack of treasure in the room. At least he was talking. She sat down beside him. Would this be the last time that she'd sit like this with him, catching the mossy scent of his body? "My brother liked to camp in the backyard when we had one. I did, too," Lavonda said.

"Older or younger?"

"My brother? Younger. He's the baby of the family. Thought I told you that." Lavonda leaned back against the boulder. Silence fell. The night sounds of the desert, including the coyotes, lulled her into a place between waking and sleeping. A good place.

His voice startled her. "What do you plan to do?"

"Tonight?"

"No. When we get back to the ranch."

"Besides convincing Cat to not claw up the furniture in retaliation for leaving?" She didn't need to see him to know he'd given her a death glare. "Sorry. It was a serious question. I'll be following up with a company in Hong Kong about work there."

"Hong Kong."

She'd surprised him. "My dream job."

"It's not making cookies in a tree?"

"That's elves." The dim light of the desert and snuffling of the horses as they shifted gave the night an intimate feeling. If he didn't want to talk, she did. She didn't usually need to talk things to death, but getting back into PR had her off her game. "All this cowgirl stuff was temporary."

"You're good at it."

"It's in the blood. Not my passion, though, really. For Jessie and Danny and even Olympia—sure. Not for me." She wanted to talk and now she couldn't even string together a sentence.

"Archaeology is like that for the Kincaids. We've been at it for generations. Do you think it's a gene mutation?"

"Maybe. Mama said that Leighs had mule blood. But that was only when Daddy was being particularly stubborn."

"You are going to Hong Kong?"

"That's the plan. This position is the one I'd have given my eyeteeth and the ranch for."

"You would have?"

She'd thought he wasn't paying much attention to anything but his own misery. "When I left my last corporate job—another downsizing—I decided to rethink things. I never thought it would take so long, but first Jessie needed my help, then Olympia. There I was working with the horses again. I forgot how great, grueling and horrible it could be. It was good for me. A mental health break, I guess, is the best way to put it."

"So you've said."

"I'm really, really good at my job and I enjoy it."

"I know the feeling. After this... I might be able to be an assistant to an assistant on the next dig. Or I may go into the Sullivan business—that's Mother's family—a long line of kilt makers. Now they specialize in pet kilts. I'll send you one for Cat." He laughed... sort of.

"No one has to know."

"Gwen and Stanley know. Glasgow and Iain know. My brother won't have much choice when it comes down to it. The university has rules and procedures. Should make him happy, though. Iain can remind me he's been telling me archaeology was about the lab and the detail, not the tales. But how will anyone want to hear about the details, if not for the tales?" Jones finally turned his face toward her and, even in the shadows, she could see the earnestness and the pain. "I've tried for years to do it Iain and Father's way. After the Dolly-Acropolis, I should have returned to the fold, so to speak. Actually, I did. Then I remembered those damned journals. I just knew if I could once and for all settle the mystery of Kincaid's Cache that I could study in the way I wanted, in a new way. I'll certainly be studying in a new way. I'll be learning exactly how to make all of those pleats in a kilt."

Lavonda slowly, cautiously reached out to lay her hand softly on his steely forearm. Emotion thrummed through him. When he didn't move or flinch, she reached down and took his hand. They sat for a moment like that. Connected palm to palm. "You are a good man. Don't forget that."

"Ha."

"It's true. Not only are you a good man, you're intelligent, creative and committed. No matter what else happens to you, no one can take that away from you."

"If you say so, but I'd like to keep something like my dignity."

"Remember how I said I rode broncs?" She felt him nod. "It's a sport where you fall...a lot. I learned my dignity had nothing to do with what anyone else saw. You know how many times I landed in a steaming pile? More than I'd care to admit. But I never worried about how I looked to other people." When had she forgotten that?

"This isn't about perception, my dear. This is reality. I went on a treasure hunt like a nutter and found what I deserved. Nothing."

"You followed a story that's been a mystery for more than a hundred years. Nothing wrong with that. You didn't find anything this time."

"You act like I'll be back. My visa is being pulled and even if you can work a miracle, I don't see any support coming from my home university or even keeping my job there."

"I don't admit that because—"

"I'm not a problem to solve. A pathetic loser that you need to prop up."

She wouldn't let him pull his hand away from hers. "I don't think you're any of those things."

"I think I am." He broke their connection, got up and strode off into the dark.

She wanted to run after him. Tell him that he

wasn't anything that he imagined himself to be. Maybe he was right, though. He wasn't a problem to solve. If she wasn't in it for the long haul, then she should allow him to find his own dignity. She went back into the tent, where she wouldn't be tempted to chase him down.

JONES CHECKED ON the horses and donkey. He knew that Lavonda had already done this, but he had to occupy himself because he'd been so tempted to turn to her and take her in his arms. What a mistake that would have been. Her career and her life were getting ready to explode with possibility. His were imploding, like when they blew up those stadiums, everything collapsing in on itself. A big structure, leveled to nothing. He'd soon be less than nothing, selling pet kilts.

He did smile at the picture of the rotund Cat in a kilt. The smile fled quickly. Another twenty-four to thirty-six hours and he'd be facing a future without Lavonda... Nothing else mattered, really. Had he just thought that? Accepted that he loved her? Loved her more than archaeology? More than his own ambitions? More than himself?

"Crappedy crap." Reese flicked an ear at him. Lavonda had even changed his ability to swear. What the hell was he going to do about this? "Nothing," he said to the donkey. "An unemployed and disgraced archaeologist? Good thing we're back at the ranch tomorrow. I can clear out. She can go to Hong Kong and have exactly what she's always wanted, right?"

"Who are you talking to?" Lavonda shouted from inside the tent.

"No one." He found himself, his boots and his not-so-lucky hat outside the tent flap.

"Don't just stand there. Come in here," Lavonda said as she pulled back the tent flap, naked and smiling.

He needed to walk away. Bed down by the horses. The lantern threw shadows over her body, creating shapes and mysteries he wanted to explore. For just tonight, he would throw away his certainty that he needed to leave Lavonda alone. Her head tilted in question.

"Are you sure?"

"I'm naked and I asked you into the tent."

He moved faster than he'd thought possible, lunging through the flap and landing the two of them on the layers of air mattress.

"Maybe this is what I really came out here to find," Jones said into her ear as his hand slipped between her thighs.

"That's what she said," Lavonda whispered back. He remembered the fun. The laughter. That's what they had together. Sexual chemistry and laughter.

Jones chuckled against her neck, nuzzling his way from her collarbone back up to her mouth. He nibbled at the corner of her lips, using tiny flicks of his tongue to encourage her to open her mouth to him.

"Lavonda, my love," he breathed into her ear. She shivered with lust. "Much better than any treasure." His mouth sealed over hers so she couldn't talk, couldn't breathe for a moment. Then he moved again and they were both flying.

JONES CRADLED LAVONDA AFTERWARD. Her head fit so neatly beneath his chin as she lay sprawled on top of him. He savored every inch of her, knowing this had to be goodbye. He thought she knew the same thing. He wanted this farewell to last because he feared that being in her arms was possibly the only place he felt like himself.

Her teeth nipped unexpectedly at the hollow of his throat, just before she pushed herself up and asked, "Do you need to hydrate before we try again?"

He thrust forward, quickly finding the pace that had them both panting and gasping, until they were so close that he had no idea where he started and stopped. These minutes needed to last for an eternity. He closed his eyes tight and sucked in the scent of her and of their lovemaking, to last him a lifetime. He knew what would come next as she began to pull away from him. He made one last effort to hold on.

She cleared her throat as she wiggled away. "I'll…" She gave a little cough. "No more, Jones. We can't do this again."

He didn't pull her back. He didn't argue. He nodded and slowly turned away. "I'll bed down outside." Exactly where he belonged. He dug through his pack and pulled out the small bottle of whiskey he'd planned to celebrate with when he found the cave. Funny how quickly the best things in his life could go bad.

Chapter Fifteen

How did men do this? Lavonda wondered as she checked her always-smooth hair in the mirror. She was proposing to Jones tonight. After getting back from the unsuccessful trip, he had started packing and making arrangements for a room near the Angel Crossing outdoor arena where he would compete in its first annual Highland regional games, then go to Tucson to catch a flight to Scotland.

She'd jettisoned the idea of a green-card marriage when she'd been sure they were going to find the treasure. She knew he needed to keep searching, especially after she'd done an internet search and understood that finding Kincaid's Cache would be amazing for not only Jones but the university, too. The cache had the aura of legend, just like the Lost Dutchman's Mine or Montezuma's Gold. That kind of search and discovery would capture spots on every morning program and the evening news. From there, Lavonda could use the interest to convince both universities that Jones was a professor they couldn't live without. He could write his own ticket. For Gwen and the university, the interest could be leveraged with the alumni for more donations. The foundation of her plan was finding the cache. To find it, Jones had to stay. Of course, even if he did, she'd still be going to Hong Kong as soon as she could…after getting the job.

Her nerves, jangling like she was on the back of a bronc, didn't understand that the proposal wasn't real. There was also the little fact that he'd say yes, because what other response was there? With the green-card marriage, he could stay, find the cache and become the biggest thing in archaeology since King Tut. It only made sense and it was just a legal arrangement. *And how had that worked for Olympia and Spence? In sappy love with two kids.* Shut up, she told that smarty-pants voice in her head. She had no expectations of happily ever after. She'd be in Hong Kong. She'd tell the immigration officials that the job had been unexpected and was a temporary posting. Or something like that. She was sure Spence was right that they took these kinds of marriages seriously. But as soon as Jones made the find, he could dissolve the marriage for nonconsummation. Because they had not been and would not be consummating any more. She'd probably forget she was even married, while she was eating Chinese food and solving big PR problems in Hong Kong. No big deal. It was her gift to Jones. So most people got…what, flowers at the end of an affair? She gave out a green-card marriage. It was all good.

Her pep talk done, she blew out a long breath and wiped her palms on her white eyelet sundress. She could do this. She'd faced down a room full of cameras and the bronc known as the Back Breaker.

"Jones," she said as she neared the living room

couch that faced the moderately large flat-screen TV. Only the very top of his red head was visible. He must be lying nearly flat. His head bounced a little and there was a loud yowl.

"Damned cat," Jones said, and sneezed.

Great. Cat had just tried to literally kill him with affection. She shooed the animal out of the room, through the kitchen and outside. She wiped her hands down her skirt again as she checked for stray Cat hairs. She heard noises down the hall in the bathroom. Jones was dosing himself with allergy medicine. Follow him or wait? She strolled down the hall, as if proposing to a man was something she did every day.

Water ran in the sink and the medicine cabinet door slammed shut. She heard muttering.

"Jones?"

"Yes?"

She walked into the narrow bathroom, taking in his slightly puffy eyes. "Was Cat lying on your head?"

"What the hell was she doing in the house?"

"She snuck in. I put her outside." He stood looking at her and Lavonda nearly lost her nerve…again. "I have something to ask you."

He remained quiet. The fluorescent light buzzed and the bathroom, which had seemed adequately large before, shrank as she stared at Jones. The Arizona sun had brought out more freckles on his forearms and hands that were furred with golden-red hairs.

"Yes?" he asked again, his green eyes intent but with no warm interest.

"Jones, I know that your visa is being revoked. I will be leaving for Hong Kong soon. I spoke with Spence a while ago and I didn't think we'd need to… There's something I'd like to do for you." She should have written out her talking points and practiced them. "Marry me, Jones." His mouth literally fell open. If it hadn't been so serious, she would have laughed. "You can get your green card, stay and keep looking for the cache. It will be in name only because I'll be going to Hong Kong." *As soon as I get the offer,* she added silently to herself.

He stared at her as if she'd grown three heads. His face paled just before red streaked across his high cheekbones.

"I can get Spence to draw up a prenup that he can keep private," she added, hoping to sweeten the deal.

"Why would I want to marry you?"

That hurt. It shouldn't, but it did. "I'm trying to help you." *You dumb idiot* was implied. She plowed on. "Just because we ended…things, and you were less than honest doesn't mean I don't care for…about you. I mean. I care about a lot of people, and you're one of them."

"So solve a lie with a lie."

"It won't be a lie. We'll be married."

"Really. We'll have a honeymoon. We'll cohabitate?"

"It'll be a legal marriage, which is why I'm getting Spence involved."

"No."

"Think about it," Lavonda said, holding herself stiff. Why didn't he understand how perfect a solution this was? "Let me explain it again."

"I am a doctor of archaeology. I have an adequately firm grasp on what you're saying. You are proposing a green-card marriage so I can stay in the United States. Although I'm a bit fuzzy on what you get out of this."

"I just want to help and I can."

"This is more than 'helping.'"

"It's what I'm good at. Fixing bad situations, repairing reputations. It's what I did. What I will do… in Hong Kong."

"Except no one has hired you to do this job."

"Well, sort of. The university—"

"Has made it clear it wants nothing to do with this project or me."

"Everyone from Gwen to the president of your Scottish university will fall all over themselves to give you a job and an office as soon as you find the cache and the find gets even just a little bit of press."

"Dear Lord, woman, you know how I feel about the press. No. This will end even worse than the last time. Enough." He stared at her, his green gaze frozen.

"But this way you can prove you were right."

"Out."

"Don't say no to my proposal. Think about it overnight."

"I will not say yes." His posture softened a millimeter. "I—I'm saying no in the nicest way possible." He pushed her out of the bathroom. She stared at the flat wooden door, registering that he'd turned on the shower. She wanted to go back in there to make him listen and understand she'd fixed everything for him. She was the fixer. That's what she did. She'd fixed this for him. She'd saved Jessie's program, and she could save Jones. He deserved saving. That was her job, her purpose. If she couldn't do that, then what would she do? Even after getting downsized, she'd still been able to help. Time to regroup, she determined on the slow stroll to her quarters.

"Yee-owl," Cat demanded. She hadn't heard the animal drag her food bowl to where Lavonda now stood in the middle of the small seating area, just off the kitchenette. Cat growled her displeasure before using a paw to smack the ceramic bowl across the tile floor.

Lavonda felt tears gathering in her eyes. She was not crying because Jones had turned her down or because he'd be going back to Scotland. Or because she was leaving the ranch that had become home. Nope. It was the thought of leaving Cat.

First, though, she'd feed her. She absolutely would not break into the emergency stash of Hobnobs. Those needed to last the feline and Jones. Lavonda didn't have time to buy more because she had plans to make and implement, and lives to change. That's what she did so well for everyone. *Except yourself.*

JONES WAITED FOR the water in the shower to warm up, while refusing to replay the farce that had just occurred. His skin itched and his eyes burned in their sockets from Cat's dander. Damned animal. He stepped into the shower he had not intended to take, except it seemed the only way to make Lavonda leave after her ridiculous proposal. He'd been insulted, demoralized and… He let the water pour over him. He needed to wash away that instant he had wanted to say yes to her.

The downward slide his life had taken since finding the dolls had hit bottom now. He had been proposed to by a woman who had made it clear that she didn't love him and thought him incapable of solving his own problems.

He turned off the water and listened carefully. No noise. He wiped off the mirror and looked at himself. The swelling around his eyes had gone away. Good. One problem on his long list solved.

He combed back his wet hair with his fingers. In less than a week, he'd be back to where he started, living in his brother's shadow, with the infamy of his greatest humiliation. If only Kincaid's Cache had been where the journal had pointed. Lavonda had had it right that such a discovery would have made his career. Maybe not in the same way as his brother and father, but it would have meant he'd have the choice of universities and access to funding. Getting married to get there, though, was just mad.

"Jones, my lad, why are you lying to yourself?" Because he so badly wanted to say yes to Lavonda and it had nothing to do with Kincaid's Cache, his career or his brother. He wanted to stay in Arizona with her. She might even want the same thing. There had been something in her cartoon-princess eyes... except, if he said yes, she couldn't go to Hong Kong no matter what she said. The US government wasn't going to believe they had a real marriage if she immediately went haring off to China.

He had to leave the ranch now. Too many temptations. If he stuck around, he might give in. He'd done so many things out of character since he'd set foot in Arizona, he couldn't trust himself to not give in to the ache in his heart he was sure would end if he admitted... He wasn't admitting anything, because he was going back to Scotland to salvage what was left of his career and reputation. At least news of his search for Kincaid's Cache hadn't gotten out on the internet.

He listened at the door before going to his bedroom where he called to change his reservation. He couldn't leave the US yet. He'd promised the Angel Crossing team he'd compete with them again. He couldn't back out on that promise.

He left the ranch saying goodbye on a sticky note.

My answer is still no. You need to take the job in Hong Kong without entanglements from your old life. Good Luck. J

IN HIS HOTEL ROOM, Jones made the call he'd been putting off.

"Yes?" Iain said when he picked up.

"It's Jones."

"I know."

"I'm ringing to let you know—"

"That there was no treasure. No cave."

"There was a cave." Buzzing silence stretched out. "I'll return home shortly and need to speak with you about my position with the university."

"What about the woman?"

Jones gripped the phone hard. "I want to talk about what will be expected of me when I return."

"I want to talk about the woman. The one who has acted as your guide."

"It's not her fault I didn't find the cache."

"Just as I thought."

"Just as you thought what?" Calling Iain had been

a mistake, as usual. The man could irritate Jones with two words.

"You have feelings for her."

What the hell did Iain mean by that? "Whatever I'm feeling is none of your business." Then Jones couldn't help himself from adding, "Just because you're my big brother does not give you the right to comment on my love life."

"So you love her. Why are you coming home?"

He remained quiet because he and Iain did *not* share confidences like two schoolgirls. "I need to work on my career. To do that, I need to be in Glasgow."

"You don't."

"Are you saying I don't have a job?"

"I'm saying that you don't need to be in Scotland," Iain said in his patient older-brother voice, the one he'd used to teach Jones exactly how to use a trowel at a dig when they were eight and six.

"My visa is being pulled and my research into legumes is near enough to complete. Why wouldn't I return to Scotland?"

"If I have to tell you, then you're not as smart as you've always told me you were."

What angle was Iain playing? Their interactions had become over the years that of professional colleagues, not siblings. Certainly not anything like caring for one another or showing an interest in each other's private life.

Iain's sigh was clear even with the spotty connection. "I might have been wrong about your studies in the States and those folktales. It might be that Glasgow could use such a branch. We should be expanding our pool of knowledge, not trying to restrict it."

Wait. Had his brother just told Jones that he was right? Maybe not right, exactly, but something close to that? "What do you want me to do?"

"You don't need me to tell you that. But I will say I hope to not see you anytime soon. I'm ringing off now."

Jones stared at the phone, expecting in bad-movie style to wake up from a dream. Had his brother told him… No matter. He couldn't tie Lavonda to Arizona. She deserved to follow her dream, too, even if it was halfway around the world. He had to go back to Scotland, right? No matter that he knew now this—Arizona, the West—was as close to home as he'd get without Lavonda. How did he do that? Get a new visa? Except he'd burned his bridge with Stanley and the university. Neither Glasgow nor Iain were an option, despite his brother's new attitude. Could he become a cowhand? Isn't that what men who moved West did? Yeah, in 1880. Staying in the desert was the first decision in years that felt right. Just as it felt right when he was in Lavonda's arms. Double crappedy crap.

JONES HAD FLED like a thief in the night, but that would not stop Lavonda from fixing the disaster he'd gotten himself into. If she did that, the ache right around her heart would go away. *Keep tellin' yourself that, baby girl*, her mama's voice rang out in her head.

Spence insisted that Lavonda could not marry Jones in absentia as she'd read about in a historical romance or maybe seen on PBS about Henry the VIII.

The attorney didn't get that Jones was thinking like a cowboy rather than an academic. She needed to give him and his career a chance by giving him more time in Arizona, which equaled marriage.

Lavonda would call Olympia and get her friend to work on her husband, because that's what a professional PR barracuda did—exploited every resource they had.

"Hello, MacCormack Spice Ranch," Olympia said in a sultry voice.

"Excuse me?"

"Sorry. Going a little crazy here. The puppy just had surgery and I have to keep him, Cal and the baby calm so that the puppy doesn't rip out any stitches. The MacCormack family does not do calm well."

"Speaking of family... I've been speaking to Spence."

"No."

"You don't even know what I'm going to ask."

"He's my husband. He said you'd come up with an idea that was creative but crazy."

"It's not crazy," she corrected.

"Really? Marriage in absentia?"

"It would fix everything."

"You're definitely a fixer and you have the best of intentions. But you know what that paves? The road to *h-e*-double toothpicks." Olympia went on after the seconds-long pause. "Since I'm already in the doghouse with you, I'm going for broke. I know you were upset because Jones lied to you and the university. You need to think about why you were so upset. Really, he just didn't tell you everything, just like you've been known to do when you worked at all of those companies. Do you think there is something else going on? Like if he wasn't revealing everything to you, he might not care for you the way you do him?"

Lavonda had a quick answer for her friend. "You don't know what you're talking about. Jones and I did not have that kind of relationship." The silence on the other end of the line made her uncomfortable, giving her time to think. "He did all of this to restore his reputation, which is an excellent goal. I just want to make sure he gets that, which means staying in Arizona until he finds the…well, a very special archaeological site."

"What else? You're leaving something out."

"That's it."

"Lavonda, you've helped everyone else. You've got to help yourself now. That's all I'm going to say because you know what you need to do." Olympia hung up.

Lavonda wanted to pound the phone into dust and scream that other than the green-card wedding, she had not one solitary stinkin' clue what to do. If she'd known what to do, she would have done it.

She wandered out to the barn to visit with Cat and Reese. The university had agreed to allow her to take the two animals with her. What she was going to do with them was still up in the air since she could be on her way to Hong Kong any day now. Lavonda had been told by Gwen, now that the papers were signed, that the university would be turning the ranch over to a conservation group interested in studying solar power and the barn was being converted into a lab. There'd be no place for the creatures. The horses already had a new home. They had been good trail animals so she hadn't been surprised by that. The goat would stay to keep the brush in check. The bottom line was that she'd fallen in love with the cat and donkey and didn't want to be parted. Why was it so hard for her to just say that?

She didn't want to marry Jones for the green card or so he could stay and polish up his reputation or even find the darned cave, its treasure and archaeological fame. She wanted to fix everything for Jones because she loved him. She drew a deep breath, the first one since she'd seen the cave was empty. She had been disappointed for him because she loved him... obviously. So how did she fix this?

Maybe this wasn't a problem to fix. Instead, it might be one of those things where she had to be brave and just hold on for the full eight seconds. Yeah. That made so much sense.

She pulled in a deep breath, held it, blew it out and let herself just feel. Yep. She loved him. Damn it. What did he feel, though? He liked her. She was sure of that. Could he more than like her? Maybe.

Okay. She'd figured out one piece of the puzzle. What did that mean?

It meant that she had to put on her big-girl spurs and take a chance...a chance at humiliating herself by telling him how she felt. Of course, if he said he loved her, too, then what? One baby step at a time.

"Road trip, you two," she told Reese and Cat, who didn't even have the decency to look at her.

Chapter Sixteen

"Déjà vu all over again," Lavonda said to no one but herself as she drove up to the town of Angel Crossing's arena, home today to the dusty regional Highland games. Her Mini Cooper sighed to a stop. Pulling a trailer, even the tiny one that comfortably fitted Reese, had been a strain. She should have waited until Olympia or someone else could have picked up the animals, but Lavonda had feared losing her nerve. Jones had already rejected her… Not *her*…the fake marriage. She'd thought proposing had been tough. This time she had to put everything on the line. *Eight seconds.* She could hold on to her backbone for eight seconds to tell him how she felt and ask him to… She hadn't quite worked that out.

"Yee-owl," Cat said from her carrier in the backseat. She'd been loudly voicing her displeasure for the past thirty minutes.

After parking in what shade there was, Lavonda plucked Cat's carrier from the car and ignored the escalating yowls. Reese quickly backed out of the trailer when asked so he could be staked by a tree and near to his buddy. Lavonda fussed over the knot, working up her cowgirl cojones to make her last-ditch, Hail Mary pitch to Jones.

The Scotsman was competing again with the crew from the university so their lime green would be easy enough to spot. She walked with purpose through the parked vehicles, channeling everything she'd learned working at the big corporations. Acting with confidence gets you the worm when you never let them see you sweat. Maybe that was one of Mama's sayings? Or a deodorant commercial?

Lavonda heard the shout of voices as she got closer to the arena. One used for rodeos obviously, with the chutes, but today tricked out with everything Scottish. Bagpipes wailed and she heard the grunt of a competitor. She stopped. Dear Lord, what had she been thinking? She shouldn't be here. She should wait and—

She heard an earsplitting bray and turned to see Reese—with Cat clinging to his back—racing into the arena.

She'd tied the donkey up, with Cat locked up in her crate. How had this happened?

More shouts from the arena unstuck her feet and she raced after the animals. Reese brayed again. She added speed.

She got into the small dusty oval with bleachers on one side. Men in kilts filled the space and the little donkey raced from grasping hands. She kept her eyes on the animals. Wait. Where was Cat? The feline no longer clung to the donkey's back. No! She kept moving as the men milled and shouted. Couldn't they see that they needed to be quiet? She couldn't believe there wasn't one horseman in the entire bunch

who knew what to do. She stopped in the middle of
the arena and watched Reese buck away from grasping hands. "Stop chasing him," she shouted. No one
heard her and now the announcer was yelling over the
sound system. Great. Reese was not a rodeo animal.
The noise and the people were scaring him. She tried
to get one of the big men's attention. Finally, someone caught Reese's halter, which only made the little
donkey lash out with hooves and teeth. Men scattered.

"Reese!" She heard the familiar voice, followed by
a yowl, then another ear-piercing bray of joy. Through
the plaid and shoulders she caught a glimpse of red
hair. Jones. "Reese," he said again. "Come see your
mate." Enough men moved that she saw Jones in full
kilt and a billowing white shirt.

Another long yowl and she finally saw Cat, standing on Jones's shoulders, her front paws planted
firmly on top of his head, as if she'd found her own
personal fire tower. Reese had stopped racing and
stood staring at his favorite thing in the world: Cat.
He shook his head and glared at the men nearby. They
all stepped back but stayed in a rough circle. Good,
she thought. Everyone had quieted and now moved
slowly inward, making the circle a little smaller, herd-
ing Reese to the center. She pushed her way forward,
using an elbow to move men to the side when she
couldn't find a small enough space to wiggle through.
She finally got into the open circle.

"Reese," she said firmly. He kicked out with both
back legs to let her know that he wasn't ready to be
reasonable. She stopped and watched in disbelief as
Jones put a piece of cookie on his head to keep Cat
in place. She yowled in delight—although it sounded

a lot like her cranky meow—and attacked the treat. Jones stood still, holding his hand out to Reese. She moved a little closer, watching the burro's hindquarters carefully. Reese took three steps closer to Jones, then brayed. Cat looked at her friend with slit-eyed superiority. Reese snorted and looked to his side. Lavonda feared he'd bolt again with the group so close. She opened her mouth, but Jones spoke first.

"Come on, my lad. Cat weighs a hundred stone, and she's getting spit in my hair." Lavonda sidled closer. She knew Jones had caught her movement. He put another bit of Hobnob on his head. Cat pounced and lost her balance, digging in her claws to keep from falling. Jones winced but didn't move. "Reese," Jones said. She saw a man across from her reach out his hand and she shook her head. But while Reese watched him, she got close enough and captured his halter in a smooth movement. Reese shook his head but settled, until Cat leaped away. Reese nearly jerked her from the ground, until Jones's firm grip covered hers.

He nodded over his shoulder. "Get Cat. I'll keep him in hand."

In a moment of high-noon-sun clarity, Lavonda understood exactly why she loved Jones and she couldn't let him go. Her jolly green Scot didn't need her to fix things for him. She wanted to do that for herself because she didn't know how else to show him that she cared…loved him. Her stomach sank. It was like being dropped on top of the biggest, baddest bronc.

What kind of woman thought about love like this? A cowgirl. That's who. And she wasn't running from that part of herself anymore, just like she wasn't going to run from Jones or this feeling, the scariest most wonderful feeling in the world, even though it made her just slightly nauseous. So much was riding on the next...eight seconds...because that's all the time she needed to tell him she loved him.

THE ANNOUNCER ADMONISHED everyone to get out of the ring so the games could continue. Now that Jones wasn't holding back a sneezing fit or staying out of the way of Reese's hooves, he wondered why Lavonda was here. And why did she have the menagerie with her? He kept his eye on her and the donkey even as a father with two young boys came up to apologize. They had heard Cat and Reese making a racket. They'd believed that they were saving the animals by releasing them. Jones told the kilted boys to get an adult the next time. He also told them that he'd pass along their apologies to the lady. Finally, he moved along after a quick thanks to the other competitors so he wouldn't lose sight of his pixie.

By her Mini, a tall blond man in a tilted cowboy hat leaned against a small-animal trailer as if he belonged there. Jones wanted to talk to Lavonda without an audience. He slowed and Reese brayed again, broke away and raced to him. He straightened and braced himself for the burro's enthusiastic greeting, the earlier thrashing-hooved menace gone. The animal had become particularly affectionate after Jones had saved him from the arroyo. He kept his eyes on Lavonda, even when he grasped Reese's halter to prevent him from head butting him.

"Cat's in her carrier in the car," Lavonda said, her

voice strange. "I can take Reese." She stepped forward. Reese brayed and showed his teeth.

Jones cleared his throat in a manly fashion. "He's fine. I—"

"This is the Scotsman?" asked the man with a set of his chin that reminded Jones of Lavonda. Her brother?

"What gave it away?" Lavonda asked. "The kilt or the fact that he's even taller than you."

"Nah. It's the way your face got all red. Been a long time since I've seen you blush." The man stuck his hand out to Jones. "Danny Leigh. Nice to meet you. Jones, right?"

Jones nodded and took his hand. The words were friendly, but he wasn't so sure the look in the other man's eyes was.

Lavonda stepped forward and Reese backed up. She set her feet in a don't-mess-with-me stance. "What are you doing here, Danny?"

"I'm here in my official capacity as mayor of Angel Crossing," Danny said. "What are you doing here? Thought you were all settled at Hacienda Bunuelos?"

"No." Lavonda looked away from her brother.

"Really? Jessie made it sound like you'd found a place to live. That you were going to settle down and—"

"I'm not. Okay?"

Danny turned to Jones, his eyes under the shadow of his hat brim steady and unfriendly. "What about you? What are you doing here…with her…donkey?"

"Just helping out." Jones didn't need to explain anything to this man. This was between him and Lavonda.

"I know you're not as dumb as you're acting right now, Danny. Move along. Nothing to see here." Lavonda didn't look as confident as she sounded.

"I'm glad you admit I'm not dumb. I want to know why this yahoo followed you out here. Shouldn't he be in there, swinging his skirt?" He never moved his gaze from his much smaller sister.

Lavonda stepped into her brother. "It's a kilt and that was a childish insult. Go be mayor. Cut a ribbon or something."

"I don't like his look. I don't think I should leave you alone here with him."

Jones had had enough. "Look, mate," he said, moving into Danny's line of sight. "We don't need your permission to have a private discussion."

"I beg to differ," Danny said.

Lavonda squeezed herself between Jones and her brother. "I want to talk with Jones and, Danny, I want you to go away."

"As Arnold says, 'I'll be back.'" Danny did a slow cowboy stroll toward the arena, then said over his shoulder, "I've got a shotgun in my pickup."

Jones watched until the man was out of earshot, then turned to Lavonda, "What the hell does that mean?"

"He's just being funny."

"Doesn't sound very funny to me."

"Danny has a strange sense of humor."

They stood in silence. Now that he was here face-to-face with her, all the words that he'd imagined he'd say were gone, sucked down into the dark pit of swirling fear that had replaced the space under his breastbone.

Lavonda resettled her cowgirl hat on her head. "Why did you leave that stupid note?"

"I didn't want to leave without saying something?"

"Crap answer. Try again."

An announcement rang out from the grandstand. He couldn't understand one word of it. When he tried to speak with her, his brain worked like Swiss cheese—holey and moldy. "I..." Crappedy crap. "I didn't want you to sacrifice the job you'd been waiting for to fix my situation. Because immigration would expect us to live together if we got married."

"I see. So, I don't have the ability to make my own decisions. I am so besotted with you that I can't think straight. Is that what you're saying?"

"Maybe?" The band inside his hat didn't stop the trickle of sweat that ran down the side of his face.

"You were able to decipher a coded journal and you can't tell me what you meant?"

"No?"

"No what?"

"Have mercy, woman. The code was nothing compared to...compared to...trying to tell you how I feel after you asked me to marry you, then said you'd run off to Hong Kong. You don't want to ever see me again, obviously. Why would I stick around to say goodbye to someone who had—"

"Don't say used you for sex. Because you enjoyed that as much as I did."

He might not be so much afraid now as mad. "This isn't about the sex."

"Then what's it about, because I thought that's all we had—sex and guide services."

"Then you aren't the cowgirl I thought you were.

I'll put Reese in the trailer. I assume you're getting rid of him and Cat so you can go to China?"

"You know what they say when you assume?"

What the hell was she going on about now? He yanked on Reese's halter to get the donkey moving.

"Stop," Lavonda said. "I came here because… I would have said this to you if you'd stayed at the ranch."

He kept moving. Any more revelations and he might have to punch something.

"I love you, you stupid Scotsman."

THAT WASN'T EXACTLY how she'd planned to tell him, but he was walking away. She had to stop him. It had worked. He stood still, scarily still.

"Pardon?" His hoarse question got drowned by a roar from the arena.

She'd said it once, and she could say it again, except he hadn't said that he loved her. Time to go big or go home…or to Hong Kong. "I love you, Jones." Now it was quiet enough to hear Reese nibbling on his lead rope.

Jones settled his hat, resquared his shoulders and turned back to her. "I thought that was what you'd said, except you were clear the only reason you wanted to marry me was so I could get a green card, find the cache and get good press for the university."

"That was right. I wasn't going to marry you because I loved you."

He looked up into the bright desert sky. Lavonda didn't move, even though she wanted to run. She'd made a fool of herself. Obviously. He still hadn't said how he felt.

"Why?"

"Why what?"

"Why do you love me? Why did you wait until now to tell me—when I leave for Scotland tomorrow?"

"You leave tomorrow?"

"Don't dodge the question," he said, his fists clenched tightly at his side and his gaze leveled on her, the Clint Eastwood squint somewhere between threatening and uncaring.

"I just do." *Lame.*

"If that's your answer, then I wish you well in Hong Kong." He looked hard at her and she couldn't open her mouth. He turned slowly, head low.

"Because you look really sexy in a kilt," she shouted after him. His step hitched but he didn't stop. "Well, damn," she muttered to herself just as Reese let out a forlorn bray. She raced after him. "Because you make me feel like the only woman on earth and then you make me feel like Bathsheba, Beyoncé and Cinderella all in one. Because when I'm with you it's better than staying in the saddle for eight seconds and even better than telling the press to buzz off."

"Bathsheba?"

"Mama made us go to church."

Just at the entrance to the arena, he turned around to her and his face wasn't in its usual lines of serious good humor. "I...I'm on my way back to Scotland where I probably don't have a job or career. I've nothing to—"

"What do you mean you've got nothing? You're a cowboy." He shook his head and she reached out slowly to touch his arm. "Yes. You are. You protect those who need it—just ask Reese. You do what needs to be done, but you're not afraid to take a risk. I've already told you that I can fix—"

"That's exactly it. I don't want you to 'fix' anything. I don't want that from you."

"Then what do you want?" She didn't hear the crowd, and she could care less that Reese was braying his head off.

"I just want to love you," he ground out, not sounding happy. "Except that—"

Lavonda ran the two steps to him, jumping up to wrap her arms around his neck, and her legs around his waist. "No *except*. You love me. You said it and can't take it back. I love you. That's all we need."

His arms, his lovely caber-tossing arms, wrapped around her, holding her against him. "That's not real. That's a song title."

"Jones," she whispered, bringing her lips to his. "I love you. It's just that simple." She kissed him long and deep.

"Wait. Stop." He set her back onto the ground. "You said I was a cowboy."

"Of course you are, because I'm a cowgirl and a cowgirl can only fall in love with a cowboy. Face it, Jones, you're stuck with me. You're stuck with Cat and with Reese."

"You didn't say anything about…wait…what do you mean stuck?"

"We're all coming to Scotland with you. I know there's quarantine or something, but I can't leave them."

"This is exactly why you shouldn't be trying to fix everything. I don't want to live in Scotland. Never did."

"Really?"

"Nope, little lady," he said, trying on a spaghetti Western accent that made her giggle. "I found a good piece of land and a good woman."

"The ranch—"

"I'm speaking symbolically, Lavonda. I don't care where exactly we settle our boots as long as it's together at the foot of the same bed, even if it's in China, although how you'll get a donkey and cat into the country... But I'm sure if anyone can do that, it's you."

"Except, I won't be taking that job. It's not me anymore. Danny told me there's a tour company for sale in Angel Crossing. I'm interested."

"For archaeologists who can't find their way?"

"Whatever it is, *we* decide together."

She stared into his green eyes and knew that whatever they did after today would work out because they were together. She'd never have to hear the words again—not that she wouldn't want to hear them—but just looking into his dear face, she knew he loved her.

"I love you," Jones said, pulling her back to him. Maybe she really did want him to say the words. Even without one *r*, he made those three little words the sexiest and sweetest in the English language.

"Yo, Jones, we need you for the—"

"Hell," Jones muttered against her lips, letting her move slowly from his arms.

"Sorry to interrupt, but we're getting ready for the *maide leisg*."

"No way, lads. I've got more important—"

"What's the holdup?" Lavonda's brother, Danny,

asked, his walk loose but his eyes intent. "I turn my back for one second… What's going on?"

"Nothing," Lavonda said quickly.

"Jones," a teammate interrupted again. "We've got to go."

Then the man she loved, the Scottish cowboy, turned to her brother. "I love your sister and we plan to…" His words dribbled to a stop. Lavonda held her breath. He would not propose. Not here. Not in front of her brother and a kilted nerd.

"Go compete," she said, pushing him toward the arena.

Danny said quickly, "No, I want to hear what he's got to say."

"I was just going to say *live in Arizona.*"

Lavonda refused to be disappointed.

"Really," Danny said, looking at the two of them. "That'll make Mama happy. Now, let's get this Scottish rodeo moving."

Jones surprised Lavonda with a deep and thorough kiss to a hoot from his teammate.

"That's my sister," said Danny.

"I have a nice comfortable bed in my motel room, which is where I'd like to be right now, making love to you, but needs must," Jones said.

"That's what she said," Lavonda whispered against his lips for one more kiss.

Chapter Seventeen

Jones scanned the crowd for Lavonda as he waited for the next set of games. She waved her fingers at him. He didn't even worry about shaming the kilt when he returned the wave.

"Jeez. How are we going to intimidate the other team when you do that?" grumbled one of his teammates.

He didn't care. He almost didn't care that he didn't have a job or much of a reputation—though that stung a bit. He'd make it up to her because that's what a man who was in love did. No doubt about it.

"Time to go, gentleman," the team captain said.

During the next break in the competition, Jones was surprised to see Lavonda's brother waiting for him.

"Since Lavonda is being Lavonda, I'm going to ask you. What's going on between the two of you? And don't try that 'nothing' crap." Danny didn't raise his voice, but his menace was clear. "Do you love her?"

"Your sister is an adult, as am I. I do not believe—"

"That was an easy yes or no question, pardner." Danny didn't make it sound like Jones was his "pardner."

"Few questions are as binary as—"

"Now you're just tryin' to show off for the dumb cowboy, ain't ya?"

Jones tightened his lips to keep himself from saying what he really wanted to. After all, this man might just become his brother-in-law. *Shite.* "I'm not showing off. I was only pointing out—"

"Ain't polite to point." Danny interrupted again.

"My first-year students have more manners than you. If you would stop—"

"So, doc." Danny made the title sound like an insult. "What's it goin' be? Yes? Or no? You love my sister, don't you? And if you say yes, I won't believe it until you prove it."

"I don't need to prove anything to you. This is not the Wild West where I have to get your permission to court your sister."

"Court? I think things may have gone beyond courting." Danny's eyes weren't visible in the shade thrown by his hat. "Plus she's got Mama and Daddy to make sure you do the right thing."

Was Lavonda the only sane one of the bunch? "I need to get ready or the next—"

"From the things I've heard from Jessie and Olympia, I think you have a lot to make up for. Do you think getting her a diamond is going to do that? Nope. You need to make a grand gesture. Like those guys you see on morning TV. So what are you going to do?"

"I'm going to act like a mature adult."

"Bad plan. I know my sister." Danny let the silence go on until it was more than uncomfortable. "So, do you want my help or not?"

"Why would you help me?" This setup sounded and felt suspicious.

"She's my sister, man."

That was the first sincere thing he'd said so far. Jones could listen to Lavonda's brother. It was polite and he did want to be on good terms with her family. Here might be a good place to start.

"LADIES AND GENTLEMEN, we have a very special competition coming up."

A few claps. She stared at Jones, in his kilt, now paired with his lime-green T-shirt with the slogan: Professors Do It With Class. He was alone, though. His teammates and other competitors stood around the arena, smiling but quiet.

"Wait, folks," the announcer said. "I've just received information about an ancient Scottish tradition. Apparently, when a man and woman compete in a *maide leisg—*"

There was a crackling in the PA system. "Well, folks, this is how it is. When a woman challenges a man to *maide leisg...*" What the heck was Danny doing on the microphone? "She determines if she'll have the man by winning the competition."

Jones remained in the middle of the arena, the toes of his restless cowboy boots kicking up little puffs of dust.

"So you may ask what happens if a lad challenges a lassie," Danny's voice boomed.

"No, we weren't wondering," Lavonda muttered.

"If the *lassie* bests him, he's required to marry her. But if he wins, he'll remain a bachelor all of his days. I don't make the rules, folks." The crowd laughed and cheered. "So, we have a competitor who would like to issue a challenge to a lassie."

Crappedy crap crap. Lavonda knew where this was headed and stood up to leave.

"There she is, folks. Ready to meet her husband... or not." The people around her cheered and wished her luck.

The crowd shouted louder. She looked down at Jones, standing tall, a light breeze stirring the edge of his kilt. She remembered the first day she'd seen him and wondered what was under it. She knew now. His gaze stayed on her and then he smiled. The big dummy was ready to be humiliated in front of all of these people who already had their camera phones out.

"Go," said a middle-aged cowgirl. "I'll film it for you. It looks like you have your work cut out for you."

Lavonda's gaze was drawn back to Jones's glinting red hair and the steadfastness of his taut jaw. "What am I doing?"

"You're going to wrestle with your true love. That's what the mayor said."

"The mayor is a—"

Danny's amplified voice cut her off. "Don't leave him in suspense. You know what happens if the woman refuses to take the challenge? She gets warts and her knees bow. Better hurry."

Why was she hesitating? Jones was the man she wanted to be with, not just today or tomorrow, but forever. He knew that, right? He knew he didn't have to make some grand gesture.

"Since I'm a mayor in the great state of Arizona," Danny said breathlessly as he raced down the bleachers with a portable mic in his hand, "I can officially oversee this ancient handfasting ritual."

Lavonda froze. She'd already made light of getting married once. She wouldn't do it again.

Danny now stood beside Jones, who grabbed the mic from him and spoke.

"There will be no handfasting. That's incorrect."

Lavonda hurried forward. She had a say in what would happen to her.

"Fine. Fine, but I see the two lovebirds are ready, so gentlemen..." Danny said, motioning to kilted bystanders who brought a stick.

She shook her head as Jones took back the mic and spoke again. "I don't like to be the center of attention and I hate having videos taken." He glared at the stands filled with people holding up phones. "But I will do all of this to prove to Lavonda Leigh that I love her."

Her throat closed as tears gathered in her eyes.

"I'm not much of a cowboy, but she's the kind of cowgirl any man would be proud to call his own." He smiled and hot tears streamed down her face. He wasn't supposed to be this romantic. He was supposed to be a stodgy egghead.

"So?" one of the men in a kilt asked softly. She used the sleeve of her shirt to wipe her eyes.

"I'm going to beat him at the...the...*may...*"

"*Maide leisg.*"

"Yeah, that." She moved forward, not taking her eyes from Jones.

"I heard it, folks," her brother announced. "She has taken the challenge."

The other men in the lime splendor of kilt and T-shirt helped Lavonda get positioned, seated in the arena dirt, with her feet against Jones's and each of them holding the same long smooth stick parallel to the ground, like they were rowers on the same oar and facing each other. They didn't talk. They didn't need to.

One of the nearby men explained whichever competitor was forced to stand up as they pushed against their feet and pulled against the stick was the loser.

"Get on with it," someone shouted.

"The public has spoken. Are you two ready?"

Lavonda nodded grimly, because she was winning this fair and square. She didn't want Jones to be in any doubt. With a grunt she pulled against the bar and braced her feet against his. She heard the crowd roaring as the two of them struggled. Well, she struggled. Her gaze locked on his green one filled with happiness, like the best-Christmas-ever happiness.

"Pull a little harder, darlin'. We have to give them a good show," he said in his awful cowboy accent, moments before he stood up and allowed himself to be pulled over and onto her.

"She won, folks," she heard Danny announce. "You know what that means? That cowboy in a kilt will be hog-tied to her forever."

"That sounds right, doesn't it?" Lavonda asked Jones, laid out along his body, not embarrassed that they were in front of hundreds of people.

"You won, all right," Jones said, rolling his *r* in that delicious way she loved. He tasted her lips and his hand pulled her close. She resisted nibbling at Jones's lips because they were in the middle of an arena with the entire—

Danny pulled Lavonda to her feet. She reached toward Jones and said, "Stop it. Let me go." She tried to pull free of her brother's grip.

"Say hi to Mama and Daddy, Lavonda. Wave."

"Don't be funny, Danny," she whispered.

He said into the microphone, "Modern technology is a wondrous thing. We were able to live broadcast this touching scene—" he swept an arm to her and Jones, who had gotten to his feet and loomed behind her "—to our parents and friends. With them as witnesses, as well as all of you, and with me in my official capacity as mayor, I pronounce the two of you man and wife. And since you've already kissed the bride, I believe my new brother-in-law should tell everyone why he loves my sister."

"Danny, what are you doing? And what do you mean—"

"Lavonda," Jones said, taking her hands in his and pulling her around to face him. The look of love in his gaze took her breath away. "I love you—anything else we can solve together."

Jones waited for Lavonda to say something. She always said something. Her cartoon-princess eyes shone brightly, sparkling with tears. His heart stopped for a second. He was sure that she was crying and about to tell him no, to tell him that this idea he and her brother had concocted had been stupid. Then a smile curved her clever mouth.

"I love you, too, Jones… Ross Nigel Meredith Kincaid."

He needed her in his arms again. He dragged her close, crushing her near enough that he didn't know where she started and where he ended. "Your pixie dust enchanted me."

A laugh rippled through Lavonda, and Jones felt more than heard her words, "Good thing I've got a lifetime supply, because that's how long I expect you to stick around."

"A life plus forever."

"Yes. A life plus forever."

He kissed her again, gently taking her lips, lifting her to him so that she fit along him in the spaces created just for her.

"Lavonda girl." He heard a woman's voice come booming over the sound system. He kept Lavonda tight against him even as she tried to wriggle away. He was glad he was wearing a sporran because she had managed to—

"That's Mama. Danny really did it." She pulled away. Jones wanted to grab her back, but Lavonda's chin had pushed out and her eyes narrowed—the look that told everyone to not mess with her.

He watched her stalk over to her brother and saw his...well, hell, the man was his brother-in-law holding out a phone in front of him like a shield. He guessed their mother was on that phone.

No matter what, Jones was not allowing Lavonda to get out of this ceremony. They were married. They could go to the courthouse or registry or wherever and make it official.

"Is Jessie there, too?"

"Lavonda, this is Daddy," interrupted a slow, drawling voice. "Put that Scotsman on the phone."

"We're not on a phone, Gerald," Lavonda's mother said. "It's Facechat. Tell him, Jessie."

"It doesn't matter, woman," the man went on, his voice being picked up by the microphone. "I want to talk with that foreigner. Danny, get him on—"

"Gerald," the woman interrupted. "You can talk with them later. See all of those people waiting for something to happen. Just tell them that we're happy, but until we give our blessing this marriage is not official. Danny, I know you're mayor and you can marry anyone, but I'm your mother and I say this one isn't official. You just take it back until we can—"

A loud whinny came over the PA system. "Dear Lord, no," Jones heard Lavonda whisper, and turned to her.

"What?"

"That pony is a menace. She's horned her way into two weddings—she is not going to be a part of a third. Who knows what she'll demand."

"I don't care. We're already married. Your brother said it's official."

She picked up his hand and squeezed. "Danny, give me the microphone." She held out her hand and her gaze was steady on her brother.

"It really was Jessie and Olympia's idea," her brother said, holding out the microphone and backing up.

"One day, you'll be in the same boat and I'll treat you as well as you've treated me." She took the microphone, but kept holding Jones's hand as she turned to the crowd.

Jones really didn't hear what she said because her pixie dust filled his ears and he only had eyes for her. He knew that he was in way over his head, and today felt almost like the day he'd fallen into the arroyo, unreal and wonderful at the same time. How could a day that started out so badly turn out so well?

He didn't care what spin she was putting on today's events, as long as at the end of it she couldn't get out of the marriage. Enough. They needed to talk privately. He might also have other reasons for wanting to be private. He plucked the microphone from her hand, gave it to Danny, then picked her up in his arms. She gave a little squeak before putting her arms around his neck. "I'm carrying you across the threshold."

"No, you're not, because this isn't where we live."

Danny's voice came across the sound system. "Folks, you have just seen another ancient Scottish ritual usually reserved for the eyes of DNA-tested Scots. It's the reenactment of the kidnapping of the first Queen of Scotland who was reported to be a pixie."

"What have you been telling Danny?" Lavonda asked, struggling now to get out of his arms. He didn't stop moving as he adjusted her weight and tightened his grip.

"It could be true."

"No one called me pixie until you showed up, and I'm not sure I like it."

"You like it just fine, and I think your brother may be more Scots than I am—which as you know is a high compliment, indeed."

"Put me down," she finally said after a brief kiss on his neck.

He ignored her comment and walked to her mobile pixie unit of the Mini Cooper and the tiny horse trailer. He put her down still in the shade but away from the carrier that he knew contained Cat.

"Jones," Lavonda said. "Are you sure? I know that Danny shamed you into—"

"My brother-in-law did no such thing." He watched her, a bright smile lighting every inch of her face. "The only thing that I want to do is love you for the rest of our lives."

"Jones," she whispered. "Me, too." She lifted herself onto her toes and pulled his head down so their mouths met in their own vow. One that said no matter what happened, they would face it together. Neither of them would be on their own anymore.

After a final soft kiss, Jones pulled himself away because he knew that they had a lot to talk about. The kissing was great and saying they loved each other was even better. All of that would make what they had to figure out possible.

"I guess I can get my green card now."

"I guess so," Lavonda said. "So you want to stay in Arizona?"

"Maybe. But that's not what you want. It might take time to straighten things out in Scotland, but are you positive you don't want to go to Hong Kong?"

Her rich brown eyes sparkled with the beginning of tears. He hadn't meant to make her cry. She shook her head and spoke quickly. "No Hong Kong. That's not for me. Maybe it would have been for that young girl running away from the boots and the saddles. That's not me anymore."

"I don't want to stand in your way."

"You won't. You'll be standing beside me." She liked that idea. "I'll need help if I try and make a go of the tour company in Angel Crossing. But first we go to Scotland for you to get straight with the university and to talk with your brother."

She really meant it, even though giving up Hong Kong and staying here made no sense. And yet it made perfect sense. Talking with Iain, though... "We'll see. Who will look after Reese and Cat?"

"Covered. Olympia or maybe Danny. They both owe me."

"You're not upset about the *maide leisg* and the phone call?"

"No. It'll be quite a tale to tell our wee ones. Is that right? Isn't that how the Scots say it?"

He laughed because many a Scotsman on telly said that. He didn't care. For now, he would enjoy the warmth in his heart. He wouldn't look for any troubles, except— "I don't have a job and probably not a career."

"What do you mean? You'll be my co-guide. Did you think I intended to do that all by myself? And we'll offer the Kincaid Cache tour. That'll give you a chance to keep looking for the secret treasure." She smiled so broadly he was nearly blinded by her happiness.

"That's what she said," he whispered, just before gently kissing her.

* * * * *

Read on for a sneak preview
of ONCE A RANCHER by
#1 New York Times *bestselling author*
Linda Lael Miller,
the first title in her brand-new series,
THE CARSONS OF MUSTANG CREEK.

CHAPTER ONE

SLATER CARSON WAS bone-tired, as he was after every film wrapped, but it was the best kind of fatigue—part pride and satisfaction in a job well done, part relief, part "bring it," that anticipatory quiver in the pit of his stomach that would lead him to the next project, and the one after that.

This latest film had been set in a particularly remote area, emphasizing how the Homestead Act had impacted the development of not just the American West, but the country as a whole. It had been his most ambitious effort to date. The sheer scope was truly epic, and as he watched the uncut footage on his computer monitor, he *knew*.

160 Acres was going to touch a nerve.

Yep. This one would definitely hit home with the viewers, new and old.

His previous effort, a miniseries on the Lincoln County War in New Mexico, had won prizes and garnered great reviews, and he'd sold the rights to one of the media giants for a shitload of money. Like *Lincoln County*, *160 Acres* was good, solid work. The researchers, camera operators and other professionals he worked with were the top people in the business, as committed to the films as he was.

And that was saying something.

No doubt about it, the team had done a stellar job the last time around, but this—well, *this* was the best yet. A virtual work of art, if he did say so himself.

"Boss?"

Slater leaned back in his desk chair and clicked the pause button. "Hey, Nate," he greeted his friend and personal assistant. "What do you need?"

Like Slater, Nate Wheaton had just gotten back from the film site, where he'd taken care of a thousand details, and it was a safe bet that the man was every bit as tired as he looked. Short, blond, energetic and not more than twenty years old, Nate was a dynamo; the production had come together almost seamlessly, in large part because of his talent, persistence and steel-trap brain.

"Um," Nate murmured, visibly unplugging, shifting gears. He was moving into off-duty mode, and God knew, he'd earned it. "There's someone to see you." He inclined his head in the direction of the outer office, rubbed the back of his neck and let out an exasperated sigh. "The lady insists she needs to talk to you and only you. I tried to get her to make an appointment, but she says it has to be now."

Slater suppressed a sigh of his own. "It's ten o'clock at night."

"I've actually pointed that out," Nate said, glancing at his phone. "It's five *after*, to be exact." Like Slater himself, Nate believed in exactness, which was at once a blessing and a curse. "She claims it can't possibly wait until morning, whatever 'it' is. But if I hadn't been walking into the kitchen, I wouldn't have heard the knock."

"How'd she even find me?" The crew had flown

in late, driven out to the vineyard/ranch, and Slater had figured that no one, other than his family, knew he was in town. Or out of town. Whatever qualified, as far as the ranch was concerned.

Nate looked glumly resigned. "I have no idea. She refused to say. I'm going to bed. If you need anything else, come and wake me, but bring a sledgehammer because I'd probably sleep through anything less." A pause, another sigh, deeper and wearier than the last. "That was quite the shoot."

The understatement of the day.

Slater drew on the last dregs of his energy, shoved a hand through his hair and said, "Well, point her in this direction, if you don't mind, and then get yourself some shut-eye."

He supposed he sounded normal, but on the inside, he was drained. He'd given everything he had to *160 Acres*, and then some, and there was no hope of charging his batteries. He'd blown through the last of his physical resources hours ago.

Resentment at the intrusion nibbled at his famous equanimity; he was used to dealing with problems on the job—ranging from pesky all the way to apocalyptic—but at home, damn it, he expected to be left alone. He needed rest, downtime, a chance to regroup, and home was where he did those things.

One of his younger brothers ran the Carson ranch, and the other managed the vineyard and winery. The arrangement worked out pretty well. Everyone had his own role to play, and the sprawling mansion was big enough even for three competitive males to live in relative peace. Especially since Slater was gone half the time anyway.

"Will do." Nate left the study, and a few minutes later the door opened.

Before Slater could make the mental leap from one moment to the next, a woman—quite possibly the most beautiful woman he'd ever seen—stormed across the threshold, dragging a teenage boy by the arm.

She was a redhead, with the kind of body that would resurrect a dead man, let alone a tired one.

And Slater had a fondness for redheads; he'd dated a lot of them over the years. This one was all sizzle, and her riot of coppery curls, bouncing around her straight, indignant shoulders, seemed to blaze in the dim light.

It took him a moment, but he finally recovered enough to clamber to his feet and say, "I'm Slater Carson. Can I help you?"

This visitor, whoever she was, had his full attention.

Fascinating.

The redhead poked the kid, who was taller than she was by at least six inches, and she did it none too gently. The boy flinched. He was lanky, clad in a Seahawks T-shirt, baggy jeans and half-laced shoes. He looked bewildered, ready to bolt.

"Start talking, buster," the redhead ordered, glowering up at the kid. "And no excuses." She shook her head. "I'm being nice here," she said when the teenager didn't speak. "Your father would kick you into the next county."

Just his luck, Slater thought, with a strange, nostalgic detachment. She was married.

While he waited for the next development, he let

his gaze trail over the goddess, over a sundress with thin straps on shapely shoulders, a midthigh skirt and a lot of silky, pale skin. She was one of the rare titian types who didn't have freckles, although Slater wouldn't be opposed to finding out if there might be a few tucked out of sight. White sandals with a small heel finished off the look, and all that glorious hair was loose and flowing down her back.

The kid, probably around fourteen, cleared his throat. He stepped forward and laid one of the magnetic panels from the company's production truck on the desk.

Slater, caught up in the unfolding drama, hadn't noticed the sign until then.

Interesting.

"I'm sorry," the boy gulped out, looking miserable and, at the same time, a little defiant. "I took this." He glanced briefly at the woman beside him, visibly considered giving her some lip, and just as visibly reconsidered. Smart kid. "I thought it was pretty cool," he explained, all knees and elbows and youthful angst. Color climbed his neck and burned in his face. "I know it was wrong, okay? Stealing is stealing, and my stepmother's ready to cuff me and haul me off to jail, so if that's what you want, too, mister, go for it."

Stepmother?

Slater was still rather dazed, as though he'd stepped off a wild carnival ride before it was through its whole slew of loop de loops.

"His father and I are divorced." She said it curtly, evidently reading Slater's expression.

Well, Slater reflected, that was good news. She did

look young to be the kid's mother. And now that he thought about it, the boy didn't resemble her in the slightest, with his dark hair and eyes.

Finally catching up, he raised his brows, feeling a flicker of something he couldn't quite identify, along with a flash of sympathy for the boy. He guessed the redhead was in her early thirties. While she seemed to be in charge of the situation, Slater suspected she might be in over her head. Clearly, the kid was a handful.

It was time, Slater decided, still distanced from himself, to speak up.

"I appreciate your bringing it back," he managed, holding the boy's gaze but well aware of the woman on the periphery of his vision. "These aren't cheap."

Some of the F-you drained out of the kid's expression. "Like I said, I'm sorry. I shouldn't have done it."

"You made a mistake," Slater agreed quietly. "We've all done things we shouldn't have at one time or another. You did what you could to make it right, and that's good." He paused. "Life's all about the choices we make, son. Next time, try to do better." He felt a grin lurking at one corner of his mouth. "I would've been really ticked off if I had to replace this."

The boy looked confused. "Why? You're rich."

Slater had encountered that reasoning before—over the entire course of his life, actually. His family *was* wealthy, and had been for well over a century. They ran cattle, owned vast stretches of Wyoming grassland, and now, thanks to his mother's roots in the Napa Valley, there was the winery, with acres of vineyards to support the enterprise.

"Beside the point," Slater said. He worked for a

living, and he worked hard, but he felt no particular need to explain that to this kid or anybody else. "What's your name?"

"Ryder," the boy answered after a moment's hesitation.

"Where do you go to school, Ryder?"

"The same lame place everyone around here goes in the eighth grade. Mustang Creek Middle School."

Slater lifted one hand. "I can do without the attitude," he said.

Ryder recovered quickly. "Sorry," he muttered.

Slater had never been married, but he understood children; he had a daughter, and he'd grown up with two kid brothers, born a year apart and still a riot looking for a place to happen, even in their thirties. He'd broken up more fights than a bouncer at Bad Billie's Biker Bar and Burger Palace on a Saturday night.

"I went to the same school," he said, mostly to keep the conversation going. He was in no hurry for the redhead to call it a night, especially since he didn't know her name yet. "Not a bad deal. Does Mr. Perkins still teach shop?"

Ryder laughed. "Oh, yeah. We call him 'The Relic.'"

Slater let the remark pass; it was flippant, but not mean-spirited. "You couldn't meet a nicer guy, though. Right?"

The kid's expression was suitably sheepish. "True," he admitted.

The stepmother glanced at Slater with some measure of approval, although she still seemed riled.

Slater looked back for the pure pleasure of it. She'd be a whole new experience, this one, and he'd never been afraid of a challenge.

She'd said she was divorced, which begged the question: What damn fool had let *her* get away?

As if she'd guessed what he was thinking—anybody with her looks had to be used to male attention—the redhead narrowed her eyes. Still, Slater thought he saw a glimmer of amusement in them. She'd calmed down considerably, but she wasn't missing a trick.

He grinned slightly. "Cuffs?" he inquired mildly, remembering Ryder's statement a few minutes earlier.

She didn't smile, but that spark was still in her eyes. "That was a reference to my former career," she replied, all business. "I'm an ex-cop." She put out her hand, the motion almost abrupt, and finally introduced herself. "Grace Emery," she said. "These days I run the Bliss River Resort and Spa."

"Ah," Slater said, apropos of nothing in particular. An ex-cop? Hot damn, she could handcuff him anytime. "You must be fairly new around here." If she hadn't been, he would've made her acquaintance before now, or at least heard about her.

Grace nodded. Full of piss-and-vinegar moments before, she looked tired now, and that did something to Slater, although he couldn't have said exactly what that something was. "It's a beautiful place," she said. "Quite a change from Seattle." She stopped, looking uncomfortable, maybe thinking she'd said too much.

Slater wanted to ask about the ex-husband, but the time obviously wasn't right. He waited, sensing that she might say more, despite the misgivings she'd just revealed by clamming up.

Sure enough, she went on. "I'm afraid it's been quite a change for Ryder, too." Another pause. "His dad's military, and he's overseas. It's been hard on him—Ryder, I mean."

Slater sympathized. The kid's father was out of the country, he'd moved from a big city in one state to a small town in another, and on top of that, he was fourteen, which was rough in and of itself. When Slater was that age, he'd grown eight inches in a single summer and simultaneously developed a consuming interest in girls without having a clue what to say to them. Oh, yeah. He remembered awkward.

He realized Grace's hand was still in his. He let go, albeit reluctantly.

Then, suddenly, he felt as tongue-tied as he ever had at fourteen. "My family's been on this ranch for generations," he heard himself say. "So I can't say I know what it would be like having to start over someplace new." *Shut up, man.* He couldn't seem to follow his own advice. "I travel a lot, and I'm always glad to get back to Mustang Creek."

Grace turned to Ryder, sighed, then looked back at Slater. "We've taken up enough of your time, Mr. Carson."

Mr. Carson?

"I'll walk you out," he said, still flustered and still trying to shake it off. Ordinarily, he was the proverbial man of few words, but tonight, in the presence of this woman, he was a babbling idiot. "This place is like a maze. I took over my father's office because of the view, but it's clear at the back of the house and—"

Had the woman *asked* for any of this information? No.

What the hell was the matter with him, anyway? Grace didn't comment. The boy was already on

the move, and she simply followed, which shot holes
in Slater's theory about their ability to find their way
to an exit without his guidance. He gave an internal
shrug and trailed behind Grace, enjoying the gentle
sway of her hips.

For some reason he wasn't a damn bit tired anymore.

Don't miss ONCE A RANCHER
by Linda Lael Miller,
available April 2016
wherever HQN books and ebooks are sold.

American Romance®

Available May 10, 2016

#1593 THE TEXAS RANGER'S FAMILY

Lone Star Lawmen · by Rebecca Winters

When Natalie Harris's ex-husband is killed, Kit Saunders is called in to investigate. The Texas Ranger quickly learns that Natalie and her sweet infant daughter are in danger...and he's the best man to protect them.

#1594 TWINS FOR THE BULL RIDER

Men of Raintree Ranch · by April Arrington

Champion bull rider Dominic Slade loves life on the road. But Cissy Henley and her rambunctious twin nephews need a man who'll stick around. Will he give up the thrill of the arena to be the father they need?

#1595 HER STUBBORN COWBOY

Hope, Montana · by Patricia Johns

When they were teens, Chet Granger destroyed Mackenzie Vaughn's relationship with his brother—or so she thought. But it turns out the noble rancher, now her next-door neighbor, may have had the best of intentions...

#1596 A MARRIAGE IN WYOMING

The Marshall Brothers · by Lynnette Kent

As a doctor, Rachel Vale believes in facts, not faith. Which is why there can be nothing between her and the town's cowboy minister, Garrett Marshall. The only problem is that Garrett believes the exact opposite...

REQUEST YOUR FREE BOOKS!
2 FREE NOVELS PLUS 2 FREE GIFTS!

⟨♦⟩ **HARLEQUIN®**

American Romance®

LOVE, HOME & HAPPINESS

YES! Please send me 2 FREE Harlequin® American Romance® novels and my 2 FREE gifts (gifts are worth about $10). After receiving them, if I don't wish to receive any more books, I can return the shipping statement marked "cancel." If I don't cancel, I will receive 4 brand-new novels every month and be billed just $4.74 per book in the U.S. or $5.49 per book in Canada. That's a savings of at least 12% off the cover price! It's quite a bargain! Shipping and handling is just 50¢ per book in the U.S. and 75¢ per book in Canada.* I understand that accepting the 2 free books and gifts places me under no obligation to buy anything. I can always return a shipment and cancel at any time. Even if I never buy another book, the two free books and gifts are mine to keep forever.

154/354 HDN GHZZ

Name _____
(PLEASE PRINT)

Address _____ Apt. #_____

City _____ State/Prov. _____ Zip/Postal Code _____

Signature (if under 18, a parent or guardian must sign) _____

Mail to the **Reader Service:**
IN U.S.A.: P.O. Box 1867, Buffalo, NY 14240-1867
IN CANADA: P.O. Box 609, Fort Erie, Ontario L2A 5X3

Want to try two free books from another line?
Call 1-800-873-8635 or visit www.ReaderService.com.

* Terms and prices subject to change without notice. Prices do not include applicable taxes. Sales tax applicable in N.Y. Canadian residents will be charged applicable taxes. Offer not valid in Quebec. This offer is limited to one order per household. Not valid for current subscribers to Harlequin American Romance books. All orders subject to credit approval. Credit or debit balances in a customer's account(s) may be offset by any other outstanding balance owed by or to the customer. Please allow 4 to 6 weeks for delivery. Offer available while quantities last.

Your Privacy—The Reader Service is committed to protecting your privacy. Our Privacy Policy is available online at www.ReaderService.com or upon request from the Reader Service.

We make a portion of our mailing list available to reputable third parties that offer products we believe may interest you. If you prefer that we not exchange your name with third parties, or if you wish to clarify or modify your communication preferences, please visit us at www.ReaderService.com/consumerschoice or write to us at Reader Service Preference Service, P.O. Box 9062, Buffalo, NY 14240-9062. Include your complete name and address.

HAR15

American Romance®

*When Natalie Harris's ex-husband is killed,
Miles "Kit" Saunders is called in to investigate.
The Texas Ranger quickly learns that Natalie, and her
sweet infant daughter, are in danger…and he's the best
man to protect them.*

*Read on for a sneak peek of
THE TEXAS RANGER'S FAMILY
by Rebecca Winters, the third book in her
LONE STAR LAWMEN miniseries.*

"Mrs. Harris?"

Whatever picture of the Ranger Natalie may have had in her mind didn't come close to the sight of the tall, thirtyish, hard-muscled male in a Western shirt, jeans and cowboy boots.

Her gaze flitted over his dark brown hair only to collide with his beautiful hazel eyes appraising her through a dark fringe of lashes.

"I'm Miles Saunders." She felt the stranger's probing look pierce her before he showed her his credentials. That was when she noticed the star on his shirt pocket.

This man is the real thing. The stuff that made the Texas Rangers legendary. She had the strange feeling that she'd seen him somewhere before, but shrugged it off. This was definitely the first time she'd ever met a Ranger.

"Come in." Her voice faltered, mystified by this unexpected visit. She was pretty sure the Rangers didn't investigate a home break-in.

"Thank you." He took a few steps on those long, powerful legs. His presence dominated the kitchen. She invited him to follow her into the living room.

"Please sit down." She indicated the upholstered chair on the other side of the coffee table while she took the matching chair. There was no place else to sit until the destroyed room was put back together.

He did as she asked. "I understand you have a daughter. Is she here?"

The man already knew quite a bit about her, she realized. "No. I left her with my sitter."

He studied one of the framed photos that hadn't been knocked off the end table, even though a drawer had been pulled out. "She looks a lot like you, especially the eyes. She's a little beauty."

Natalie looked quickly at the floor, stunned by the personal comment. He'd sounded sincere. So far everything about him surprised her so much she couldn't think clearly.

He turned to focus his attention on Natalie. "You're very composed for someone who's been through so much."

"I'm trying to hold it together." After all, with her own personal Texas Ranger guarding her and Amy day and night, what was there to be worried about?

Don't miss THE TEXAS RANGER'S FAMILY
by Rebecca Winters, available May 2016 wherever
Harlequin® American Romance®
books and ebooks are sold.

www.Harlequin.com

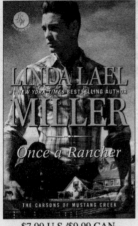

THE WORLD IS BETTER WITH

Romance

Harlequin has everything from contemporary, passionate and heartwarming to suspenseful and inspirational stories.

Whatever your mood,
we have a romance just for you!

Connect with us to find your next great read,
special offers and more.

f /HarlequinBooks
🐦 @HarlequinBooks
www.HarlequinBlog.com
www.Harlequin.com/Newsletters

HARLEQUIN®

A *Romance* FOR EVERY MOOD™

www.Harlequin.com

SERIESHALOAD2015